HOODIE ASSASSIN

Table of Contents

Chapter 1

Jark was jolted awake by the sound of creaking wood and the soft shuffle of feet. He lay still for a moment, the hazy edges of sleep retreating as his mind caught up to the fact that someone was in his room. Slowly, he blinked and sat up, squinting through the darkness to make out shapes. His heart raced, and for a moment, he wondered if this was just a bad dream.

"Who are you guys?" Jark asked, his voice cracking slightly as he saw the silhouettes of three men standing at the foot of his bed. "W-what do you want?"

The tallest of the three stepped forward, his face partially obscured by the low light streaming through the window. "We're looking for Jarkor Danga," the man said, his tone smooth, almost too calm for the situation.

Jark swallowed nervously as his heartbeat sped up. He glanced at the open window and cursed his past self for leaving it open. It must have been too easy for them to come inside.

Jark contemplated only for a moment. They didn't have any threatening weapons in their hands at the moment. If they tried anything, he could always scream for his parents. He swallowed nervously and then said, "I'm Jark. Why are you looking for me?"

The man glanced at his companions before speaking again. "We've been watching you, Jark," he said, eyes gleaming in the flash of the moonlight, "We know you've been looking for a job. Well, we've found the perfect job for you."

Jark's mind raced as he processed the absurdity of the situation. Strangers had broken into his house, watched him, and now they were offering him a job? His eyes narrowed as he took in their dark clothing, their demeanor, and the way they moved like shadows in the night.

"But you guys look like... assassins," Jark said, the realization hitting him like a cold wave.

The man nodded as if this was the most normal thing in the world, "Yeah, we are. But we need your help."

Jark blinked, "I'm just a college student. How am I supposed to help with that? You've got the wrong guy."

The third man, who had remained silent until now, took a step forward, his voice a low rasp as he spoke, "We know about the way you feel. How you wish you could eliminate some people because they're terrible. We've been watching long enough to know you're fit for this job."

Jark felt a chill creep down his spine. He wasn't sure how they knew about his dark thoughts – those fleeting moments of frustration when he imagined a world without the people who

2

made life harder. But he wasn't serious about it. He didn't mean it, not in the way they were suggesting.

"But…killing is bad," Jark said, his voice barely above a whisper. He didn't know what else to say. This wasn't just some philosophical debate in class. These were real men standing in his room, men who had probably done things he couldn't even begin to fathom.

The tall man spoke again, this time with a faint smile on his lips, "What if we told you there's a special tool? Something that makes you invisible when you need it. It makes it easier, and you'd never have to face any consequences," he shrugged, "No one would know."

For a brief moment, Jark felt a pull, a temptation to consider what they were saying. The thought of having power like that, the ability to right the wrongs he saw in the world, to eliminate the worst people without anyone knowing, sounded like something out of a fantasy. But it was wrong. It had to be.

"That sounds like a nice offer, but I have to decline," Jark said firmly. "I might get angry at people, but killing them isn't the solution."

The man's smile faded, and he exchanged a glance with the others. "Fine," he said, his voice now cold, "But just know this…the government keeps pushing out dumb rules, and innocent people are suffering because of it. You had a chance to stop them. You had a chance to make a difference, but you refused."

With that, the men turned and made their way out of his room. As they moved, one of them let something slip from his hand. It fluttered to the floor, landing with a faint rustle. Jark stood frozen for a moment, his mind spinning with the surrealness of the encounter.

"What is this?" Jark mumbled as he walked over to where the paper lay. He picked it up and called after them, moving toward his window, "Hey! Hey, dudes, wait! Assassins, or whatever you are – you forgot something!"

But they were already gone, disappearing into the night like shadows that had never been there. Jark stared out into the dark street, the silence almost eerie now that the men were gone. He glanced down at the paper in his hand and unfolded it, his heart thudding in his chest.

As he read, a knot tightened in his stomach. The words said: 'Blood floods the Red Sea, and people don't see what's going on. You have been chosen, and you must respond "yes" or you will join the sea of blood.'

Jark swallowed hard, the words echoing in his mind. "Okay, no. That's a threat," he muttered, feeling his hands tremble slightly as he crumpled the paper. He didn't want to think about what they meant by "joining the sea of blood." Whatever it was, he wanted no part of it.

He moved quickly, tearing the paper into pieces before tossing it into the trash can. The adrenaline that had been coursing through his veins began to fade, leaving behind an unsettling sense of dread. He sat back down on his bed, running his hands through his hair.

"What the hell just happened?" Jark asked himself quietly, trying to process everything. The whole thing felt like a bad dream, except the crumpled paper in his trash can reminded him it was all too real.

He took a deep breath and glanced around his room, half-expecting the men to reappear. But the house was silent now, and the only sound was the faint ticking of the clock on his desk. He lay back down and stared at the ceiling, willing himself to fall asleep again.

But as much as he tried, sleep wouldn't come. The weight of what had just happened, of what he had just been asked, hung over him like a heavy fog. He couldn't shake the feeling that this wasn't over, that the men wouldn't just leave him alone now that he had said no.

And what if they were right? What if the world really was as bad as they said, and he had passed up on the chance to change it?

Jark shook his head, pushing the thought away. He wasn't a killer. He couldn't be.

But as he closed his eyes, he couldn't help but wonder if they would be back.

Chapter 2

The next morning, Jark stumbled out of bed, his mind still groggy from the restless night before. He rubbed his eyes and stretched, trying to shake off the lingering thoughts of the strange men who had visited him. It felt surreal, like some twisted dream, but the mess they'd left in his room was all too real.

"This is outrageous. Where is my hoodie?" Jark muttered, rummaging through a pile of clothes that had spilled onto the floor. Shirts, pants, and socks were scattered everywhere, a reflection of his chaotic mind. As he searched, he couldn't help but wonder why they had trashed his room in their search for him. It still didn't make sense.

He hadn't noticed it the night before, but in the light of the day, it was clear that they had searched through the room before he woke up.

"I wonder why they even trashed my room just because they were looking for me," he mumbled under his breath absentmindedly, his frustration building.

"Who was looking for you?" His mother's voice startled him from the doorway.

Jark stood up straight, his heart racing. "Uhm, nothing. I was just talking about why I'm always scattering my room," he said quickly, forcing a nervous smile.

His mom raised an eyebrow, clearly not convinced, but she let it go. "Well, I'd like to see it neat before you leave for college," she said, her tone firm but not unkind.

"Okay, Mom," Jark replied, not wanting her to stay for too long because his mom had the uncanny ability to make him spill his guts and he didn't want to scare her by telling her about the guys who came last night.

He turned back to the mess and began shoving clothes into drawers, barely bothering to fold them. The last thing he needed right now was more questions. He couldn't explain what had happened, not to her. Not ever.

As he tidied up, his mom lingered at the door, "By the way, your hoodie is downstairs, and breakfast is ready."

Jark's face lit up for a moment. "Oh, I hope it's pizza," he said, half-joking but secretly hoping it was true.

"No, Jark," his mom replied, her voice carrying the same exasperated tone she always used when he brought up pizza for breakfast. "You can't eat pizza all the time you know?" she sighed in frustration and left the room, shaking her head though Jark knew she was smiling as well. He could hear it by the tone.

His mom acted like his obsession with pizza bothered her to no end, but in all honesty, she also indulged him a lot. And Jark was all too happy for it.

Jark sighed, half-relieved that the conversation hadn't gone deeper. He grabbed his backpack and headed downstairs, throwing on his hoodie. After a quick breakfast, he was out the door and on his way to college, trying to push the strange events of the previous night out of his mind.

At college, the halls were buzzing with the usual morning energy. Students gathered in groups, chatting about homework, weekend plans, and the latest gossip. As Jark made his way to his locker, he was greeted by a familiar voice.

"Yo, Jark, how you doing?" Kadrea called out as he approached him with his usual dopey grin on his face.

Jark turned to him, forcing a smile despite the exhaustion he felt. "You know, just…being tired," he said, trying to keep his tone light.

Kadrea snorted. "You need to start getting some rest," he said jokingly, though there was a hint of genuine concern in his eyes.

Jark shrugged, "Yeah, maybe." He wasn't ready to talk about the real reason he couldn't sleep last night. Just thinking about it made him shudder.

"So, what class are we having first?" Jark asked, changing the subject.

"Well… I need to check," Kadrea said, pulling out his phone and started scrolling through their schedule.

As they walked through the crowded hallway, the usual buzz of conversations surrounded them. Jark overheard snippets of conversations from groups of students gathered in small clusters.

"Did you hear what they said?" one voice muttered nearby.

"Yeah, we're in trouble," another replied.

"How?" asked a third, their voice filled with worry.

Jark's curiosity piqued, and as they continued toward their classroom, he leaned closer to Kadrea. "What are they talking about?" he asked in a whisper, noticing the tension in the air.

Kadrea glanced over his shoulder at the group before turning back to Jark. "I have no idea," he said, his tone thoughtful. "But I heard about a guy…someone who feels like he has friends but deep down, he feels really alone. Some people are saying he could be the new hero."

Jark felt his stomach drop, "Wow, that sounds dangerous," he said, his voice quieter now. "Those kinds of people are dangerous."

Kadrea nodded slowly. "Yeah. Now, no one's trusting anyone, but…" he hesitated for a moment before turning to look at him and said, "I trust you."

Jark felt a pang of guilt stab through him, sharp and cold. He trusted him, and here Jark was, keeping secrets from him. He tried to swallow the guilt, but it sat like a stone in his chest. "Yeah…I trust you too," he said, forcing the words out even though they felt like a lie at the moment.

As the guilt became too much to bear, Jark's mind scrambled for an escape, "Uhm, Kadrea, I think I'm going to the bathroom," he said, already taking a step back.

Kadrea tilted his head slightly and shrugged, "No problem." Kadrea waved him off casually as he continued toward their class.

Jark turned and headed in the opposite direction, feeling the weight of everything pressing down on him. He couldn't keep pretending everything was normal, not after what had happened. The men, their strange offer, and the note they left – it was all too much. He felt like he was being pulled into something dark, something he couldn't escape from, and the worst part was that he didn't know how to stop it.

And now everyone discussing about this new hero…things had started to feel a bit too real.

Chapter 3

Their math teacher droned on and on about something. Jark's head lolled to the side, and he shared a "so done" look with Kadrea. Yes, there were bigger things to worry about, but right now, Mr. Wallace's monotonous drawl was the bigger worry. It sucked all the joy out of Math.

Just when things were about to get borderline unbearable, someone in their class gasped and got up from their seat. Jark's head jerked to the girl who had jumped out of her seat to stare at the front gate of the college.

Men dressed in official garb were entering their college and Jark's eyes widened when he realized they were the CIA. But what were they doing at Jark's college?

As more people found out, chaos started erupting. Everyone got up from their seats and started to stare out of the windows to see what the CIA was here for.

Jark followed suit and found a space amongst the crowd to stare upon the approaching soldiers along with their General.

Jark was calm, observing the frantic scene that had developed in such a short span of time. It all felt surreal – the moment the CIA barged into the college, guns at their side and eyes filled with a hardened, callous determination. Jark watched the scene unravel with a mixture of disbelief and frustration. He didn't understand why they were doing this. No one did.

The General, a tall man with a gravelly voice, barked commands to his soldiers. They scoured the classrooms, shoving students aside, rifles pointed, looking for their supposed "threat."

"We are the CIA, and we need everyone out of the class now!" the General's voice had boomed, and the students, terrified and confused, had complied without hesitation. All except one – a girl, sitting quietly in the corner, almost invisible to the chaos.

"Soldiers, go and check around!" the General ordered. The soldiers fanned out, moving through the hallways, knocking down doors, and searching for something, someone. Jark had wanted to speak up, to tell them this was madness, but before he could muster the courage, one of the soldiers voiced what Jark had been thinking.

"But General, how would we find the person? It could be anyone. I can't even stand to watch this-"

A gunshot cracked through the air, silencing the soldier's complaint. The bullet had passed clean through the man's head before he even finished his sentence. Blood sprayed across the floor, and he crumpled to the ground in a heap.

The General's eyes were cold as he turned to his troops. "Now, does anyone else see a problem with my instruction?" he growled, his voice low and dangerous.

"No, sir!" the remaining soldiers responded in unison, their fear palpable.

"Good," the General gave a single nod, "Check everywhere. Anyone who doesn't seem like the others – kill them immediately."

They moved quickly after that, more ruthless than before. When they found the girl in the corner, it seemed like the end for her. The soldiers raised their weapons, fingers hovering over the triggers.

But then, in a split second, their guns were sliced into pieces.

"Who did that?" one of the soldiers shouted, his face contorting in fear as he stared at his ruined weapon.

A hooded figure stepped forward from the shadows, and with a calm but commanding voice, the cloaked figure said, "I did. Leave the girl alone. She is disabled and does not deserve to be treated like an outcast."

The soldiers hesitated. For a moment, it seemed like they might listen, but the General was not one for patience. "Kill it!" he barked, pointing at the hooded figure, "It sounds like a girl – it'll be easy!"

What followed was anything but easy.

The hooded figure moved like a whirlwind, taking down each soldier with swift, precise movements. Blades flashed, and bodies fell. By the time the figure reached the General, the ground was littered with soldiers, their blood pooling beneath them.

The General wasn't like his men. He was a seasoned warrior, protected by some kind of armor that deflected bullets and swords alike. The fight between him and the hooded figure was brutal and lasted for nearly thirty minutes. In the end, though, the hooded figure was knocked to the ground. The General stood over the fallen figure, panting but victorious. As the cloak fell away, revealing the figure's face, Jark's eyes widened in shock. The fighter wasn't a young girl, as the General had thought – it was an old man.

"You came to fight me with your puny, aging body?" the General sneered, laughing. He was about to drive his blade into the old man's chest when Jark, unable to stay silent any longer, shouted.

"STOP!"

The General paused, looking up. "What is going on here?" Jark asked, stepping forward, his voice steady despite the chaos surrounding him.

"We are looking for the Chosen One," the General replied, his tone condescending. He waved a hand dismissively toward the bodies on the ground. "These sacrifices are necessary."

Jark shook his head, his expression filled with disgust. "Is that what you call this? Sacrifices? This is murder. You're teaching these kids that violence is the solution to everything. You're making them think it's okay to kill, and then you wonder why society falls apart," he heaved a breath, then continued, "All of this is so immature. You are promoting violence by doing this in front of impressionable young teens. This is a college and now you will see students carrying a knife to come and kill someone and you will say your citizens are not good meanwhile it is the elders that have broken the way of life!"

He paused, glancing at the students who had been watching the scene unfold in horror. "Someone might be different, might feel left out, and all you're doing is fueling that isolation with more hatred and fear. You need to look at yourselves and ask if you're the real problem."

Jark's words hung in the air for a long moment. The General, still holding his blade, seemed to falter for the first time. He glanced down at the old man, who was now struggling to breathe, and something shifted in his expression.

"I'm sorry for fighting you mate but I have to be the Chosen One," the general said, his voice softer now. He extended a hand, helping the old man to his feet. But as soon as the old man stood, his body began to disintegrate, turning to dust before their eyes.

"What the…?" The General stumbled back, staring in shock as the old man's remains drifted away in the wind. The students remained still in shock as well while behind the General, the soldiers who had fallen moments earlier stirred and began to rise, their wounds gone.

"We're not dead," one of them muttered, looking around in confusion.

"What the hell is going on?" the General asked, but there were no answers. The General shook his head and said, "Well then, men, let's go!" They all filed into a line and started following the General through the hallways but as they were almost at the doors of the college, the soldiers that had seemed real started to flicker, and then they faded away into illusions.

When all his classes were over, Jark's mind was still buzzing with the day's events. Kadrea, his best friend, found him outside, helping the girl from earlier – the one who had sat quietly in the corner.

"How are you doing? Do you need help?" Jark asked, offering her his hand to help her stand.

"I'm not actually disabled," she admitted with a shy smile, "I just didn't want to be with my friends – they're mean."

"That's… that's tough," Jark said, awkwardly trying to think of something comforting. "By the way, I'm Jark."

"I'm Tabitha," she replied, smiling as someone called her name from across the yard. She waved and skipped away, leaving Jark standing there, wondering if he'd just met an angel. He could do nothing but stare at her retreating back and smile.

"Pretty girl, huh?" Kadrea said, coming up beside him.

"What? Me? No, I don't-" Jark stammered, replying to a question that was never asked.

Kadrea grinned. "Relax, I was just messing with you. But seriously, where do you want to go now?"

Jark thought for a moment, then said, "How about the mall? I need a new hoodie since I have only two left and the other ones I have were donated because they were small."

"Lead the way, man," Kadrea replied, and the two of them headed off, leaving the bizarre day behind.

Chapter 4

Jark couldn't help but marvel at the decorations scattered around the mall. Banners of bright colors, glimmering streamers, and balloons tied to railings created a festive atmosphere that piqued his curiosity.

"Wow, I wonder what's happening here with all this decoration," he said aloud, glancing at Kadrea.

"We're having a farewell party," a passerby replied nonchalantly as they strolled past.

"For who?" Kadrea asked, raising an eyebrow.

"It's not for who, it's for what," the person added before walking away, leaving Jark and Kadrea standing there, perplexed.

"Huh?" Jark and Kadrea said in unison, staring at each other in confusion.

"You're confusing us," Jark called after the stranger, but he was already gone.

Just then, another voice chimed in. "We're having sales," a woman said, standing behind a makeshift kiosk. Her tone suggested that she'd explained this a hundred times already today.

"Ohhh, that's what they meant," Kadrea said, nodding in understanding.

"Was that too hard to understand?" came a familiar voice from behind them.

Jark and Kadrea turned around, surprised to see their friend San standing there, a smirk plastered on his face as if he had been following the conversation all along.

"Where did you come from?" Kadrea asked, his tone light, but genuinely curious.

"I was just around, and I figured, why not join in on the confusion," San said with a casual shrug. He had a way of appearing out of nowhere and injecting himself into conversations, like a breeze you didn't realize had swept in.

"You weren't at college today," Jark said, eyeing San suspiciously.

San rolled his eyes. "Seriously, Jarkor, you need to loosen up. Studying isn't the whole world, you know." He shared a look with Kadrea, and the two of them broke into laughter.

Jark crossed his arms, feeling the weight of their teasing. "That's not fair," he muttered.

"Oh, I'll tell you what's not fair," Kadrea said with a mischievous grin, clearly eager to stir up more trouble.

"What is it?" San asked, already sensing there was more to the conversation.

"Jark has a crush on one of the popular girls in college," Kadrea announced with far too much enthusiasm for Jark's liking.

Jark felt his face grow warm, and he glared at Kadrea. "How do you know she's popular?" he asked, trying to deflect the attention.

"You haven't seen her Snap score, that's why," Kadrea quipped, as though that explained everything.

Jark narrowed his eyes. "How do you even know her Snap score? You're a stalker!" he accused, hoping to turn the tables.

"No, I'm not! It's just obvious that she's popular," Kadrea replied, completely unfazed.

"What's her name, by the way?" San asked, jumping in with a smirk.

"It's none of your business," Jark snapped, his embarrassment growing by the second.

Kadrea, never one to let things go, leaned closer to San and said in a mock whisper, "Her name's Tabitha."

"Hey!" Jark shouted, finally fed up. Without another word, he stormed off, his frustration bubbling over.

As he walked away, he could hear San's confused voice behind him. "What's his problem? Can't he take a joke?"

Jark didn't bother to answer. He needed a break from his friends' relentless teasing. With each step Jark took, he tried to calm down, pushing thoughts of Kadrea and San out of his mind. Soon, he found himself in front of the clothing store he had been planning to visit. It seemed like a good distraction from everything that had just happened.

"Hello, how can I help you?" the cashier greeted him as he entered.

"I want to buy a hoodie and maybe a new shirt," Jark said, trying to sound casual. "Something that matches and makes me stand out," he added, thinking he could at least feel good about himself in new clothes.

The cashier nodded and pressed a button under the counter. Another employee appeared from the back room, ready to assist.

"He's looking for a hoodie. Can you help him out?" the cashier asked.

"Sure thing," the second employee said with a smile, motioning for Jark to follow her.

As they made their way through the aisles, the employee's phone rang. She quickly answered it without breaking stride. "I know, Mum," she said, her voice tired. She kept her conversation brief, but Jark could hear muffled voices from the other end of the call. He found himself wondering what the conversation was about, though he quickly dismissed the thought.

They arrived at the hoodie section, and the employee ended the call. "Okay, Mum, I'll do it. Just stop calling me at work," she said in an exasperated tone before turning back to Jark. "Let me know if you need any help," she added before walking off.

Jark scanned the racks, picking out a few options. "At least I know my mum will send me money for this stuff," he muttered to himself as he made his way to the fitting rooms with his selections in hand.

He stepped inside one of the small cubicles and tried on the first hoodie. As he studied himself in the mirror, the lights above flickered ominously. His heart sank. "Oh no, not again," he whispered.

In the reflection, a shadowy figure appeared behind him, pointing directly at him. It was the same figure that had haunted him in moments like this before.

"I've told you before, leave me alone," Jark said, his voice strained but firm.

The figure didn't waver. "Yeah, I would, but people are suffering," the figure said in a cold, echoing voice. "Your race is treated like crap. Just because you feel segregated doesn't mean others haven't been hurt more. Look at Tabby. She's always bullied, and you're just going to let that slide?"

Jark clenched his fists, trying to push the figure's words out of his mind. "Just because you're probably a spirit or whatever doesn't mean I'm going to listen to you," he snapped, pulling the hoodie off and storming out of the fitting room.

He hurried back to the front of the store with his chosen items. "I'd like to pay for these," he said, trying to keep his voice steady as he passed the clothes to the cashier.

"That'll be twenty dollars," she replied.

Jark fumbled with his wallet, pulling out the cash. "Here," he said, handing it over.

"Thank you," the cashier said with a smile.

Jark nodded in response, grabbing his bag and making a quick exit from the store. He needed air, space, anything to shake the lingering tension that clung to him from the encounter in the fitting room.

As he stepped back into the bustling mall, he tried to put the strange reflection and its unsettling words behind him. But deep down, Jark knew that the figure wasn't going to leave him alone anytime soon.

He joined his friends again, but he still couldn't shake off the unsettling feeling.

He was jerked out of his thoughts by Kadrea loudly asking, "Why do you look down, bro? Did you not find any hoodie you liked?"

Jark blinked at his two friends, some of the fog finally leaving his mind. He shook his head and said, "I don't know-I mean, I did," Jark heaved a sigh, his shoulders slumped as he said, "Can we just go home? I'm not feeling right at the moment."

His friends looked at him weirdly but Jark marched on ahead, towards the exit.

He just wanted to go home and sleep the whole encounter with the figure away.

Chapter 5

When Jark got home, he noticed something was off the moment he opened the door. His parents were sitting in the living room, and the atmosphere felt heavy. They were talking quietly, and his dad was holding a sheet of paper, their expressions unreadable. Jark knew instantly what was about to happen.

"Hi, Mum. Hi, Dad," he said, trying to sound casual, hoping to maybe share what he'd bought at the mall, but he didn't even get the chance. His dad stood up abruptly, still gripping the paper like it was something venomous.

"What is this?" Dad asked, thrusting the report towards him. His tone wasn't just angry – it was disappointed, and somehow that stung worse.

Jark glanced down at the paper, his stomach sinking. "Uh... it's my report," he replied, already knowing where this was headed.

"Why are your grades so poor? Is this what you've been going to college for?" Dad demanded, his voice rising with each word.

"But I got an 80 out of 100," Jark said, trying to defend himself. In Jark's mind, 80 was solid. He worked hard for that grade and stayed up late studying for that stupid test. But he should've known better. Nothing was ever enough for Dad.

"And so? You're supposed to get 100. Maybe even a 101," he shot back. His eyes were cold like Jark had let him down in some profound, unforgivable way.

Jark felt something snap inside of him. He wasn't about to stand there and be made to feel like a failure when he'd done his best. "If you don't think I'm good enough, fine! You have a dumb son. Deal with it," Jark shouted, storming off before they could respond.

He slammed the door to his room and threw himself onto the bed, his chest heaving with frustration. Why was he never good enough? No matter what he did, no matter how hard he tried, it was never enough for his dad. All he wanted was to feel like he wasn't constantly disappointing them.

As Jark lay there, staring up at the ceiling, his mind began to drift. He tried to distract himself with thoughts of Tabitha or anything else, but the weight of the argument lingered, pressing down on him. Then, suddenly, a scream ripped through the house.

Jark sat up, his heart pounding. "What's going on?" he muttered, rushing out of his room and toward the sound.

The scene in the living room stopped him in his tracks. Jark's mum and dad were tied to chairs, swords pressed against their throats by shadowy, cloaked figures. His blood ran cold.

"No!" Jark shouted. "Leave them alone! What do you want from me?"

One of the cloaked figures stepped forward, their voice low and commanding when they said, "We want you to take up the offer, or else your family gets it."

"Fine, I'll join! Just don't hurt them!" Jark yelled back, his heart racing. Though he couldn't help but ask, "Why me? Why is it compulsory that I do this?"

The figure tilted their head. "Because you are the Chosen One," they said simply like that explained everything.

"The Chosen One?" Jark echoed, his mind spinning. "To kill people? I don't want to do that! But you've sent these assassins here to threaten me like this? What the hell is wrong with you people?"

The assassin holding the sword to Jark's mum's throat pressed the blade closer, and she let out a terrified scream.

"Please! Stop!" Jark cried, lunging forward, but another one of them grabbed him, holding him back.

The head of the group stepped between Jark and his parents, his voice chillingly calm as he said, "You've accepted the offer. Now, it's time for your initiation."

Before Jark could even process what was happening, they grabbed him and dragged him away from his parents. He tried to fight back, but there were too many of them, and they were strong – far stronger than Jark was.

They took him to a secret place. The walls were covered in strange symbols and pictures of people wearing hoodies, just like the ones the assassins wore. Jark glanced around, a sense of unease growing in his stomach. He didn't know how they had come here because his vision had been covered by their towering, hooded figures.

"Who are all these people?" Jark asked, his voice trembling slightly despite his attempt to sound brave.

"They are assassins who kept their word and fulfilled their oath," the Head Assassin explained.

Jark swallowed hard, his mouth dry, "And what happens to those who don't keep it?"

One of the others chuckled darkly, "You wouldn't like the answer. But don't worry – you'll find out soon enough."

They led him to the center of a circle, and Jark stopped, his gut telling him that this was not going to end well. "Am I supposed to stand here?" Jark asked, hesitating.

The Head Assassin nodded. "Yes, now step into the circle."

Jark stepped inside, feeling like he was walking into a trap he couldn't escape. "Okay, let's get this over with," he muttered, trying to hold on to any shred of control.

The Head Assassin raised his arms, and the others stood at attention. "Now, we begin," he said solemnly.

Before he could continue, Jark blurted out, "Can we not do this? Killing is a sin, you know. It's against God. There has to be another way to solve this."

The Head Assassin looked at Jark curiously. "Oh? And what would that be?"

"We could pray. Just leave it all to God. He'll sort it out," Jark said, grasping at any hope he could find.

The Head Assassin let out a dry chuckle, "Yes, but even the Bible says faith without works is dead."

Jark blinked in surprise. "Wait, you believe in God?" he asked, genuinely caught off guard.

The head nodded, "I did, and I still do. That's why I'm taking action."

"But why do I have to be involved?" Jark asked, frustration creeping back into his voice.

"Because," he said, leaning in, "you're the chosen one."

Jark sighed. "Fine. Let's just get this over with," he muttered, already regretting his decision.

"Repeat after me," the Head Assassin instructed. "I, followed by your name."

"I, Jark," Jark said reluctantly.

"Pledge to do the will of the hood or suffer the consequences," he continued.

"Uh, what exactly are the consequences?" Jark asked, feeling more uneasy by the second.

"JUST SAY IT!" he shouted, making Jark flinch.

"Alright, alright! I, Jark, whatever, pledge to do the will of this... worthless scrap cloth... or suffer the stupid consequences," Jark said sarcastically, rolling his eyes.

The room fell silent. Everyone was staring at him, murmuring among themselves.

"Quiet!" the Head Assassin barked, silencing them. "You have mocked the hood. Now, you will suffer the curses that follow."

He handed Jark a note with a name on it. "Kill this person."

Before Jark could even react, the entire room was engulfed in fog.

Chapter 6

The next day, Jark woke up with a jolt, his body still tense from the remnants of a dream he couldn't shake off. He blinked a few times, trying to piece it together, then yawned and stretched as the morning sunlight streamed into his room.

"What a dream," Jark muttered to himself as he dragged himself out of bed, heading for the mirror. He moved automatically, preparing for college. His mind was still foggy from sleep, but he had the eerie feeling that something wasn't quite right.

After getting ready, he spotted something that made his heart sink. There, on his dresser, was a piece of paper. For a moment, he froze. He knew exactly what it was before he even touched it.

"Oh no…it wasn't a dream," Jark whispered, dread sinking deep into his chest. Trembling slightly, he unfolded the paper and read the mission that he was supposed to accomplish. His eyes skimmed over the cold, merciless words.

"No, no, no…Must I do this?" Jark groaned, staring up at the ceiling as if it might provide some divine intervention. "I said I don't want to kill anyone! Please, choose another chosen one," he pleaded to the empty room, his voice low and desperate. But he knew there would be no answer. The weight of the responsibility had already been placed on him, and the consequences of defying it were far worse than he could imagine.

Later at college, Jark did his best to act normal, but it wasn't easy. He was constantly on edge, trying to shake the unsettling thoughts that clung to him like a shadow. As he approached his friends, he forced a smile onto his face.

"Hey dude," San said, his voice light and easy as he greeted Jark with a slap on the back.

"Sup," Kadrea added, shaking hands with Jark. There was comfort in these familiar interactions, but Jark couldn't bring himself to fully engage. His mind was elsewhere – on the mission, on the person he was supposed to kill.

"I'm glad you're all here," Jark started the urge to confess everything suddenly overwhelming. He needed to tell someone – anyone. But then, out of the corner of his eye, he noticed someone standing near the wall, making a subtle motion for him to stay silent. His blood ran cold.

"On second thought…never mind," Jark said quickly, his voice faltering. He glanced away, feeling the mysterious figure's presence linger like a warning.

"What is it? What did you want to say? If it's about Tabby, we already know," San teased, unaware of Jark's internal struggle.

"What? No, it's not that, it's…" Jark trailed off again, his eyes darting nervously to the figure still lurking in the shadows. He felt trapped, his secret choking him. "Fine. It is about Tabby. I just… I feel like she's not into guys like me," Jark lied, hoping to divert the conversation.

"You'd never know until you try," San said, slinging an arm around Jark's shoulders in a friendly gesture.

"Good. It's time for class," Jark said, seizing the opportunity to escape the conversation as he looked at the time and realized they would be late for class if they didn't start moving. He rushed ahead, leaving his friends behind.

San frowned, watching Jark's retreating form. "I wonder what's up with him. He's acting suspicious," San murmured to Kadrea.

"Yeah, let's just go to class," Kadrea replied, though he couldn't help but feel the same unease.

In class, Jark found it nearly impossible to focus. His mind kept drifting back to the mission. He stared blankly out of the window, watching the trees sway in the wind, but his thoughts were a whirlpool of fear, guilt, and uncertainty.

"What's so special out there that you keep staring at it?" his teacher's voice cut through the haze, pulling Jark back to the present.

"Uh, nothing. Sorry," Jark mumbled, hastily turning his attention back to his work. But even then, his concentration was shattered. His friends noticed, making jokes to lighten the mood, but Jark couldn't join in.

After college, as soon as the final bell rang, Jark couldn't get out fast enough. "Guys, I think I'm going to head home. I'll see you tomorrow," Jark said, rushing off before anyone could question him further.

San watched him go with narrowed eyes. "Kadrea, we need to find out what's wrong with him."

"You read my mind, but I'm not in the mood to follow him," Kadrea replied as they both watched Jark run down the hallway toward the exit.

Jark was out of breath by the time he reached home and ran up to his room. He paced the periphery of his room, clutching the mission paper tightly in his hand. "Now I need to find this person, get the mission done, and leave," he muttered under his breath. The thought of it made his stomach churn, but he had no choice. If he didn't complete the task, the consequences would be dire.

Pulling a hood over his head, Jark felt a strange, otherworldly light surround him, signaling that the time had come. He slipped out of his house and made his way to the target's location. The night was quiet, and the shadows seemed to stretch longer than usual as if they were watching him.

When he arrived at the house of his intended victim, he climbed onto the rooftop, waiting for the lights to go out. His heart pounded in his chest. So, this is my first mission, he thought, swallowing the lump in his throat. I hope I can get this over with.

He didn't know why they had chosen him for such a task, or why they hadn't trained him properly, but it didn't matter. If he didn't do it, they would kill him.

Eventually, the lights went out, and Jark knew it was time. He moved like a shadow, slipping into the building and dispatching the guards as quictly as he could. Finally, he was face-to-face with the man he had been sent to kill.

"What do you want from me? Please, leave me alone," the man, Smay, pleaded.

"I'm sorry, but what you've done to people is unforgivable. They've ordered me to put you to sleep," Jark said, his voice hollow, detached.

"But I have a family. That's why I do what I do," Smay tried to reason, desperation in his voice.

"Yeah, yeah. Let's just finish this," Jark muttered, just as more guards burst into the room.

"Freeze!" they shouted, surrounding him.

Jark's mind raced. "I don't think so," he growled, fighting them off with a flurry of movements he hadn't even known he was capable of. When the dust settled, the guards were down, but Smay had escaped.

Jark chased him outside, only to find Smay slumped against a wall, an arrow lodged in his chest. "Please, save me, and I will reward you," Smay begged, his voice weak.

Jark hesitated for only a moment before shaking his head. "Sorry, but I have a job to finish," he said, and with one swift motion, he ended Smay's life. A strange sense of satisfaction washed over him, followed quickly by guilt.

"That felt…nice," Jark said to himself, pulling off the hood. But then he realized what he had done. "Oh wait, I'm supposed to leave first," he muttered, quickly slipping the hood back on and vanishing into the night.

Unbeknownst to Jark, a man watched the entire scene through a hidden camera. His face was obscured, but a sinister grin twisted his lips. "I'll get you, Jark. Or should I say, Hoodie Assassin," the man whispered, rubbing his hands together as he chuckled deeply, utterly satisfied by what he had seen.

Chapter 7

The next day at college, Jark felt the weight of guilt and confusion pressing heavily on his chest. He hadn't slept much after what happened the previous night, and his mind was still racing, filled with dread. Every step he took toward the college building felt as if it might be his last. He was trapped in a nightmare of his own making, one he couldn't escape.

As he walked through the hallway, trying to avoid the gazes of his peers, he heard a familiar voice behind him.

"Hey, Jark, have you seen Kadrea?" San asked, his tone casual as though it was just another ordinary day.

Jark froze for a moment, the blood draining from his face. "No, have you?" he replied, his voice unsteady.

"Seriously, if I had, I wouldn't be asking you," San said, frowning slightly. He didn't notice Jark's distress, but he could tell something was off.

"Oh, sorry," Jark muttered, trying to regain his composure.

"Why are you apologizing?" San asked, his brow furrowed in confusion.

"I have no idea," Jark said quickly, distracted by the sight of Kadrea approaching from the other end of the hallway. Relief and fear washed over him in equal measure.

"There he is," Jark pointed, and both he and San made their way toward Kadrea.

As they neared him, Jark could immediately sense something was wrong. Kadrea's face was dark, his expression unreadable, and his eyes held a fury Jark had never seen before.

"Kadrea, what happened?" San asked, concern creeping into his voice.

Kadrea's gaze flickered between San and Jark, then settled on Jark with a cold, calculating glare. "I just found out my uncle was killed last night," Kadrea began, his voice low and ominous. "And it was the Hoodie Assassin who did it."

Jark's stomach dropped, dread turning his limbs to lead.

San got closer to Kadrea, putting a hand on his shoulder, and asked, "Do you know who is the Hoodie Assassin?"

Kadrea's eyes flickered towards Jark and in that moment, Jark knew that Kadrea knew exactly who the Hoodie Assassin was.

Jark moved quickly, pushing San away light and pulling Kadrea to the side. "Come with me," he said tightly, his heart pounding as he pulled Kadrea away from the crowd and out of the college.

He didn't care that San was calling after them, he didn't care that their class was most likely to start, he only cared about Kadrea and what he knew.

Jark didn't stop until they were at the back of the college where barely any students wandered. Only then did he let go of Kadrea and turned to face him.

Kadrea's face was like stone, and his eyes emotionless.

Jark breathed deeply and said, "Do you know?"

Kadrea's eyes hardened the moment Jark spoke. Anger, frustration, and helplessness flashed into his eyes. He stalked closer to Jark and harshly whispered, "What do I know?" He chuckled darkly.

Jark swallowed, his throat feeling dry when he choked out, "A-about the Hoodie Assassin."

His palms were sweating and he could feel more sweat pooling at the base of his neck. He felt like he would pass out at any moment.

Kadrea snarled and lunged towards Jark, pulling him in by the collar as he glared at Jark harshly. "It's you, Jark. The Hoodie Assassin is you. Is that what you wanted to hear? Did you get some kind of sick satisfaction from hearing me say that? Are you happy that you killed my uncle?"

"No," Jark said, trembling as words tumbled out of his mouth in a gasp, "I swear, Kadrea, I didn't-"

"You didn't what?" Kadrea snarled again, his anger boiling over.

Jark took a deep, calming breath, and then blurted out, "No, it wasn't my fault!" His words came out in a rush as he went on to say, "I couldn't make a choice! It was either me or him! I'm sorry!" he pleaded, but the words felt hollow even to him.

Kadrea wasn't listening. His hand was already reaching into his jacket, and Jark watched in horror as Kadrea pulled out a gun. "You killed my uncle, Jark," Kadrea said, his voice trembling with rage. "I trusted you. I told you everything. We swore we'd never hurt each other, and you broke that promise. Now, this is your end."

Kadrea reloaded the gun and raised it towards Jark.

Jark's heart pounded in his chest. Every fiber of his being screamed for him to run, but he couldn't move. His legs were frozen in place, and his mind was spiraling out of control. He didn't want to die, but the sight of Kadrea's furious face made him feel as if he already had.

"I trusted you, Jark," Kadrea hissed, his voice shaking with fury and grief. "You were my brother. But now, you're just a murderer. Everyone is going to know about what you did. Do you think I'm the only one who knows? You don't know the half of it. You're going to die, and I'm going to tell everyone what you did. And if not me, then someone else might leak your dirty secret. One way or the other, you're over, Hoodie Assassin. Sooner or later, every bod will be aware of your true face. This is the end for you."

Kadrea aimed the gun squarely at Jark's chest. Just as he was about to pull the trigger, something snapped inside Jark. The hood covered his face in a blur of shadow. Jark felt his body move without his control as the hood transformed him into something else – something darker, something unstoppable.

With lightning speed, Jark's body leaped forward, a blade appearing in his hand. He slashed through the gun with ease, sending it clattering to the ground. In one swift motion, he pointed the blade at Kadrea's throat, the metal glinting in the fluorescent lights.

"You work against me, and you die," Jark said, his voice layered with an unnatural double tone that sent shivers through the crowd of onlookers.

Kadrea didn't flinch. He stared defiantly at Jark, his breath shallow and his chest heaving. "Go ahead. Do it," he whispered.

For a moment, everything seemed to freeze. The world slowed, and Jark felt the blade in his hand tremble. He didn't want to do this. He didn't want to kill his best friend.

But the hood had other plans.

Before Jark could stop it, the blade plunged into Kadrea's chest. Time snapped back into motion as the world erupted into chaos. Kadrea gasped, his eyes wide with shock and pain. Blood poured from the wound, and Jark could only watch in horror as his friend collapsed to the ground.

"No! What have I done?" Jark cried, stumbling back as the hood withdrew from his face. He dropped the blade and knelt beside Kadrea, frantically pulling the sword from his chest. "I'm sorry! I didn't mean to! I'm so sorry, Kadrea!" Tears filled his eyes as the crowd around them swarmed, pushing him away from Kadrea's lifeless body.

How could he do this? Jark thought, putting his head in his hands. Jark didn't have an answer to that. He couldn't explain the darkness that had taken over, the uncontrollable force that had driven him to this horrible act.

Jark couldn't bear to stay any longer. He bolted from the scene, running as fast as he could, not caring where he was going. There weren't many students loitering about but the ones who were still outside blurred together as Jark tore through the hallways, their voices fading into the background. All he could hear was his own ragged breathing and the pounding of his heart.

Later that night, Jark lay curled up on his bed, his body shaking with sobs. He couldn't stop thinking about Kadrea – the look in his eyes, the way his body crumpled to the ground. The blood. The betrayal.

"How does a man cry for doing the right thing?" a voice said, and Jark looked up to see the figure of the hooded figure sitting at the foot of his bed. It was the Head Assassin of the group that had broken into his room the first time.

"I didn't want to kill him," Jark whispered, his voice hoarse from crying. "He was my friend."

The Head Assassin shrugged casually, "He was going to be next anyway. You saved yourself some trouble."

"What do you mean?" Jark asked, his voice trembling.

The Head Assassin leaned in closer, its eyes gleaming from the shadows, "Remember the oath you took? The one you joked about? That's the consequence. You kill people close to you because the hood is still in charge."

Jark clenched his fists, anger rising within him. "Why didn't you tell me this sooner? Why didn't you warn me?" he shouted.

The hooded figure chuckled darkly, "You didn't ask. But it doesn't matter now. It's time for the silencer."

"What does that mean?" Jark asked, his stomach twisting with fear.

"You're going to kill yourself in front of everyone at college," the hooded figure said, its voice cold and emotionless.

"Why would I do that?" Jark asked, utterly lost.

The Head Assassin sighed, "Your best friend is dead, Jark. His body was found at the back of your college. And when they ask who was the last person seen with him, they're all going to point at you, Jark. They already know the Hoodie Assassin is a part of your college, it's only a matter of time before the death of your friend and his uncle is traced back to you."

Jark didn't know what to say. He was shell-shocked like someone had pulled the Earth from beneath his feet.

Seeing his hesitation which must be written all over his face, the Head Assassin continued, "What do you think they will do once they find out you killed your best friend? No one would even want to talk with you. They wouldn't even want to look at you. The police will investigate his death, and the truth will come out," he sighed, "I would say, save yourself from this misery and execute your own death in front of your college before someone else does that for you."

"Why does it need to be in front of everyone?" Jark asked in a low voice.

The Head Assassin chuckled darkly, "Well, you don't want them to keep looking for you for years to come now don't you?"

Before Jark could react, the Head Assassin vanished, leaving Jark alone in the dark.

The next day, Jark walked into college with a heavy heart. He sought out San, who was standing with a group of students.

"Hey, San," Jark said, his voice low.

San looked at him with a morose expression on his face. "Jark, I looked for you everywhere. Did you know what happened to Kadrea? Everyone's talking about it. They think it's the Hoodie Assassin and that the government will be investigating to catch him out. Where were you when all this happened?"

Jark swallowed hard. "My mom called me home," Jark lied straight through his teeth, "She needed something."

San looked confused but he still nodded, but before he could ask anything else, Jark said, "It's time for my class," and ran ahead.

Jark didn't go to his class though. he ran straight up to the roof. He didn't know what to do. Everyone was already talking about the Hoodie Assassin and if they investigate, then Jark would be the first person they come to.

Jark paced on the roof, running his hands through his hair as he came to the realization that the Head Assassin was right.

He had to do it and he had to do it in front of everyone.

Jark waited up on that roof until most of the classes were over. He knew that by seeing the number of people coming out of the college building.

He took a deep breath and then he leaned forward to fall.

A hand grabbed him from behind. "You can't die on college property," a voice said, "The college would be held responsible."

Jark looked at the figure, their face obscured. "Fine," Jark muttered, "I'll write a suicide note." Then, without hesitation, he jumped.

As he fell, he felt a strange sense of relief. "At least I don't have to do this anymore," he whispered just before his body hit the ground.

The news about Jark's death spread like fire.

The noise coming from the television was interrupted by a woman's sobs.

"This is the saddest thing to happen a teenage boy just committed suicide because he felt bad for himself-" the news lady was saying, a somber expression on her face.

Jark's mother sobbed as his father said, "I can't believe our son is dead." There was disbelief in his voice like he couldn't accept that this was their reality.

"My son is gone because of me," Jark's mother wailed, remembering her son's sweet and innocent face.

How could such a devastating thing happen?

Chapter 8

At the Assassin's Society for boys, Danse, the head of the assassin's society, spoke with triumph. "Yes, we've finally made them get rid of him. Now we must seize this opportunity and place our people in power," he declared.

Gera, the advisor, voiced his concern. "But sir, we need more recruits, and no one is joining," he said as Danse paced silently. "Sir?" Gera repeated, trying to catch his attention.

Danse paused, deep in thought. "I'll figure something out, but with that annoying hoodie-wearing assassin out of the way, we can strike," he said confidently. He then pointed toward the busy workers. "Hey, you! Get those trucks loaded. We're going hunting," Danse ordered with determination. The time to act had finally come, and the society was ready to take control.

***

Hego, the head of the assassins, entered a dimly lit room, his steps soft and deliberate. The air was heavy and thick with the smell of old wood and something darker. In the center of the room lay a body, motionless and cloaked in shadows. Hego knelt beside it, his movements slow, almost reverent.

His lips moved in a whisper, speaking words that even the keenest ear could not decipher. These were not words meant for ordinary hearing, but something ancient, secret.

Once he finished his incantation, Hego stood, his face as expressionless as ever, though there was a lingering weight in his eyes. He turned and left without a glance back, his mind already elsewhere.

In a vast, open space that seemed to stretch infinitely, Jark found himself standing alone. The air felt unreal, dense with an unsettling silence. He took a few cautious steps forward and called out, "Hello... Anyone here?" His voice echoed back at him, repeating over and over until it faded into the void.

"Where am I?" Jark asked aloud, feeling his pulse quicken. Everything was strange, foreign. His eyes darted around the expanse, searching for anything familiar, but there was nothing. "Am I... in heaven?" he wondered aloud.

But something about the place didn't feel right. Heaven, as he'd always imagined, was supposed to be bright and peaceful. This place, this vast emptiness, felt hollow and eerie.

"Wait," he mumbled, his thoughts scrambling. "No, this isn't heaven. Heaven is warm and safe. This... this feels wrong." His thoughts spiraled as he looked around the void, a creeping dread crawling up his spine. "Am I in hell?" The idea seized him, his breath quickening. Panic began to set in. "No, Lord, please. I'm sorry. They forced me to kill. I didn't want to. I'm innocent," the words tumbled out desperately as if some distant force might hear him and offer a reprieve. But nothing answered him except the haunting silence.

He stood there, hands trembling, feeling more lost than ever. "If I'm dead, how can I repent?" Jark's voice cracked as the weight of the situation pressed down on him. His fear deepened as his surroundings refused to change, refused to offer him any clarity. "Hello!" he shouted again, hoping, praying for any response.

In the distance, a shadow moved. It was barely perceptible but unmistakably there. Jark squinted, trying to make out the figure, but it was shrouded, its form unclear. Was it a person? A statue? He couldn't tell, but his heart raced at the possibility of not being alone.

"Hello?" he called out again, more hopeful this time.

A voice answered though it seemed to come from all directions at once.

"Hello."

Jark froze. "Who are you?" he asked, his voice a mix of curiosity and fear.

"Who are you?" the voice echoed back, identical to his own words. Before Jark could say more, the figure darted away, vanishing into the distance like a wisp of smoke.

"Wait!" Jark shouted, his legs springing into action as he began to chase after it. "Aren't you a person?!" His feet pounded the ground as he ran, trying to keep up with the fleeing figure. "Wait – you're a girl, aren't you?" His breath was coming fast now, more out of desperation than exertion. The figure ahead was slipping away, becoming harder to see, and his heart raced with the fear of losing it.

Suddenly, the figure stopped dead in its tracks, forcing Jark to come to a halt too, nearly stumbling from the suddenness of it. The silence around them grew louder, heavier.

"Where are we?" Jark asked, panting.

The figure turned slowly, and in an instant, Jark's heart dropped. It wasn't a girl anymore. It wasn't even someone else. It was him. His own face stared back at him, distorted and cruel.

"Where are we?" his Echo mocked, its voice perfectly mimicking his.

Before Jark could react, his Echo reached out and shoved him hard. The ground beneath Jark's feet disappeared, and he tumbled backward into an abyss. "How is this place a mountain?" he yelled, confusion mixing with terror as he fell. The walls around him morphed, turning into a cave, then a waterfall, until he was plunging through rushing water. His stomach lurched as he neared the river below, the world spinning uncontrollably.

Then, with a shock, he was awake.

Cold water splashed over his face, jerking him from the dream. Gasping, Jark shot upright. "Hey!" he yelled, blinking rapidly to clear his vision. "What was that for?"

Hego stood above him, holding an empty bucket. "You've been asleep for three days," he said, his voice flat and matter-of-fact, "Your body needs food. If you don't eat, you'll die for real."

Jark rubbed his face, trying to process what had just happened. "Wait! How am I not dead?" His mind raced, trying to piece together how he could possibly be alive after everything he'd experienced.

Hego's gaze was steady when he said, "Because you have the hoodie."

Jark blinked in confusion and asked, "What?"

Hego sighed, as if explaining something obvious, "We needed a way to make you leave your family. To train you. The hoodie protects you."

"You made me leave my life just for this?" Jark's voice wavered between disbelief and anger. "I didn't want this. I didn't ask for any of this!"

Hego remained unmoved, "Normally when teens get powers, they're excited. Why aren't you excited?"

Jark stared at him, his jaw clenched as he spoke through gritted teeth, "Because I'm not like other teens. I didn't want powers. I wanted a life." He paused, frustration boiling over. "What else can this hoodie do?"

A faint smirk tugged at the corner of Hego's lips. "I could tell you," he said, "but where's the fun in that?" Without waiting for a response, he turned and began walking away.

Jark stood there, frozen for a moment, before shouting after him. "You can't just leave me! I don't have any life left anymore!"

Hego merely pointed to a table set up nearby, laden with food. Jark hadn't even noticed it until now. His stomach growled loudly, reminding him of how long it had been since he'd eaten. Without thinking, he rushed over to the table and began shoving food into his mouth.

"This is huge," he mumbled between bites. But even as he ate, a sinking feeling remained. What had he become? And what was waiting for him next?

***

At home, the atmosphere was thick with sorrow and tension. "Oh no, what have I done for my son to do such a thing?" Jark's mother cried, her voice trembling with regret. She was being comforted by her husband and daughter, Daisy, while the middle child, Kule, sat nearby playing a game, seemingly indifferent.

"You're the reason he left anyway. You tried to control his life," Kule said, his eyes fixed on the screen.

"What? How can you say that?" their mother asked, hurt flashing across her face.

Kule shrugged, pausing the game, "You don't get it. You want your children to grow, but you can't let them go into the real world. You think sitting and waiting for God to fix everything will work. Didn't you teach us that God helps those who help themselves? If we don't, how will He help us?"

His mother was stunned, speechless.

"It's okay, Mum. I'm here for you," Daisy said softly.

Kule scoffed. "Yeah, like you're the replacement for our older brother."

Daisy shot him a glare. "Why aren't you bothered that he might be dead?"

Kule shrugged again as he stood to leave. "I don't feel like he is," he muttered before heading to his room.

Chapter 9

Jark sat in the worn leather chair of the therapist's office, his head resting in his hands, eyes heavy with guilt. He tried to explain, though words barely scratched the surface of the horror he carried.

"Not only that," Jark muttered, his voice low, "but once I was sent on my rest missions, it reached a point where I didn't want to do it anymore. I was tired. So I killed them – all of them. Trust me, it was brutal." His eyes, shadowed by the weight of his memories, flickered as flashes of how it all went wrong played in his mind like a cursed reel of film.

The therapist, Doctor Zanda, listened quietly. She wasn't a stranger to cases involving trauma, but something about Jark's situation unsettled her. She knew there were layers to his story that even he didn't fully understand.

"How do I save myself, Doctor?" Jark finally asked, a raw vulnerability cutting through his voice.

Doctor Zanda tapped her pen against her chin thoughtfully before responding, "We could try reconnecting you with your family. Sometimes going back to those who love you most can-"

"Even if that works," Jark interrupted, shaking his head, "there's still the voice I hear in my head. Every single day. It's loud, and controlling, and it never stops. It's…it's annoying."

Doctor Zanda frowned as she walked around her desk, looking for a particular file. "This is a serious case," she admitted, "In all my years of practice, I've never heard anything quite like this."

Jark stared at the ceiling, his voice growing bitter when he said, "What makes it worse is that now, this is my life. No family, no lover, no friends. Nothing. I'm completely alone."

He gave a half-hearted laugh, but there was no joy in it. "I don't even know how I was able to pay for this session," he added, more to himself than to her.

Dr. Zanda raised her eyebrow, noticing the despair woven into Jark's words. "Have you tried removing the hoodie?" she asked cautiously, referring to the mystical garment that had been bonded to him since his life as a regular boy had unraveled.

Jark let out a frustrated sigh, "I have, but it's only when I shower that the hoodie lets me be. It's like it's alive…and it won't leave me."

The therapist paced thoughtfully before making a suggestion, "Perhaps we could try taking it off now – if that's okay with you."

Jark shrugged and told her, "I don't see why not."

As Doctor Zanda approached, something strange happened. The atmosphere in the room shifted, and the light outside the window dimmed unnaturally. The sky itself seemed to darken, clouds swirling in a spiral above the building, twisting like some malevolent omen.

Jark felt a coldness creep into his mind. His eyes narrowed as he felt the presence, the voice in his head – the voice of the hoodie. It wasn't just inside his head; it was speaking through him now.

"Why are you trying to take me off my host?" Jark's voice rumbled, but it wasn't entirely his own. The voice was layered, deeper, more menacing, as though someone – or something – was speaking through him. "He is the chosen one," it continued.

Doctor Zanda froze, momentarily startled. She steadied herself and faced the voice that wasn't Jark's. "Have you ever considered," she began calmly, "that he doesn't want to kill people? That he's trapped by you?"

The voice inside Jark scoffed, "And who are you now, his mother? Do you think you know what's good for him better than I do?"

"No, I'm not his mother," Doctor Zanda replied, trying to stay composed. "But you should-"

Before she could finish her sentence, a blade materialized from nowhere, sharp and gleaming, slicing through the air in a swift, merciless motion. It passed cleanly through Doctor Zanda's neck, her eyes wide with shock as she collapsed to the floor, blood pooling beneath her.

Jark gasped, his consciousness snapping back into control. He stared down at the body of the only person who had tried to help him. "No!" he cried, horrified, "What have I done?"

The hoodie pulsed around him, its sinister grip tightening on his soul. "I really wish I'd used those two years wisely," Jark muttered bitterly, wiping a streak of blood from his face. "Now, there's no way I can master this stupid thing. It keeps forcing me to kill innocent people."

As he spoke, Jark heard footsteps approaching from behind. Instinctively, he turned and swung his sword, his weapon slashing through the air with deadly precision. But his attack was blocked by something, or rather someone.

Claw Fist, a brawler known for his brutal strength, stood before him, unfazed by Jark's sudden attack. His metallic claws gleamed as they extended from his fists. "Nice speed, dude," Claw Fist said, smirking.

Jark's eyes narrowed as he sized up the stranger. "You remind me of someone," Jark said cautiously, feeling a strange familiarity in Claw Fist's demeanor.

"If you're thinking of Wolverine, then yeah, I get that a lot," Claw Fist replied, a sly grin spreading across his face, "But I'm not him. We have different goals, different powers."

With lightning speed, Claw Fist launched himself forward, throwing a punch aimed straight at Jark's face. Jark barely managed to block it, but the sheer force of the impact sent him staggering back.

"I see you're not like the rumors say you are," Claw Fist said, his tone more curious than accusatory.

"What rumors?" Jark asked, his breath labored.

Claw Fist laughed darkly, "Oh, you really want to know? Let's just say the world sees you as a cold-blooded killer. But me? I think I'm better than anything they said about you."

Without warning, Claw Fist threw another punch, this time with even more power. The force of the blow sent Jark crashing into the wall, the impact leaving him momentarily winded.

Jark groaned, clutching his ribs, "How…how are you this strong?"

Claw Fist shrugged, his claws retracting slightly, "I eat my vegetables."

Just as Claw Fist was about to deliver the finishing blow, a voice boomed through the building's shattered windows, "This is the police! You are under arrest. We have you surrounded. Don't try anything funny!"

Claw Fist glanced at Jark, then at the police outside, "Well, I guess that's my cue to leave. Too bad – I was really looking forward to killing you."

He helped Jark to his feet, a strange camaraderie passing between them for a brief moment. "Next time, though," Claw Fist promised, flashing a sharp-toothed grin, "I'll finish the job."

"Wait!" Jark called out as Claw Fist sprinted toward the exit. "Who are you?"

Claw Fist paused at the door but didn't turn back. He simply continued running, disappearing into the shadows before the police stormed the building.

Inside, the captain barked orders to his squad. "Split up! They were spotted here. We need to find them before they escape."

Minutes later, one of the officers found Doctor Zanda's lifeless body, the sight sending a wave of horror through the team. "Captain!" the officer shouted, "We found Doctor Zanda. She's dead."

The captain cursed under his breath. "This isn't good," he muttered. "They must want something else."

"What else could they want?" asked one of the officers, his voice trembling.

The captain shook his head. "I don't know. But whatever it is, it's bigger than this."

Later, the captain stood before General Maddy, his expression grim. "Ma'am," he said quietly, "We lost them again."

General Maddy's face was stoic, but her eyes betrayed a steely resolve. "We'll find them," she said with certainty, "Sooner or later, we'll get them."

Chapter 10

Jark blinked, still disoriented from the sudden shift in his surroundings. He remembered being cornered by the police, hiding among the trash to escape, and then – nothing. Now, here he was, in his apartment, as if he had teleported here.

"How did I get here?" Jark whispered, his voice hoarse, eyes darting around his dimly lit room.

"Calm down. It's okay. Don't stress yourself," a voice soothed from somewhere in the room. "Let the Kaderian cloth do its magic."

Jark's eyes narrowed, instinctively reaching for the hoodie that never left his body. "You mean the hoodie, right?" he asked.

"Yes," the voice answered simply.

Jark turned toward the source and saw a figure, a woman, sitting casually on a chair near the window. He hadn't noticed her before.

"Who are you, and why did you help me?" he asked his body tense despite the calming tone of her voice. The woman had an air of control about her, something unsettling.

"Well, it's a long story," she replied with a faint smile.

Jark leaned forward slightly, curiosity mixing with suspicion. "Do tell. I like stories – at least, I think I do. I haven't heard one in five years." His voice grew bitter as he continued, "Not since I started working for them, killing for them. Two years with them, then three alone." He paused, realization hitting him. "Wait…how did you even get into my home?"

The woman, Barro, smiled again, unperturbed. "Calm yourself. Let me begin," she said, her eyes distant as she spoke, "It all started when I was 12…"

*********FLASHBACK*********

Kacey stood in the doorway of her room, hearing her mother call for her from downstairs. "Kacey, where are you?" Ciara's voice echoed through the hallway.

"I'm here, Mum," Kacey replied, stepping out and walking toward the kitchen, where her mother stood waiting. She was used to this, the silent weight that had hung over their home since her father had left seven years ago. But today, something felt different, a strange tension was present in the air.

Ciara's eyes were solemn, her expression one Kacey had rarely seen – full of unspoken sorrow. "It's been seven years since your father left us," she said.

Kacey's heart twinged. She hated being reminded of him, of the way he had disappeared from their lives without a trace, leaving her and her mother behind. "Why do you have to bring that up?

I've already forgotten," she muttered, though deep down, she hadn't. She could never forget.

Ciara, however, wasn't done. She walked over to the table and picked up a kit – an old, weathered leather case, the kind that looked like it had seen decades of use. Then she turned to her and said, "You have to man up now. It's your turn."

Kacey stared at the kit, confusion crossing her face and she asked, "Time for what? What is this?"

Her mother held it out to her, her voice shaking just slightly when she said, "You are the new Barro. And this is your bow and arrow."

Kacey recoiled, a sharp pang of fear lancing through her. "But I don't want to be! That's how Dad was killed!" Her voice was trembling now, the memory of her father's death crashing over her like a cold wave. "I don't want to die and leave you alone."

Ciara's face softened, but her voice remained firm when she spoke, "I'm sorry, my love, but Dad had to pass this down to his son. Since he didn't have a son, it has to be you," she looked down, her voice almost breaking, "I could have taken on the role, but it was meant for your father's lineage. If I tried, it could kill me. Please, Kacey, you need to do it for your father."

Tears welled up in Kacey's eyes as she clutched the kit with her hands shaking. "But Mum, I'm just a kid," she whispered, a few drops of tears escaping from her eyes.

Her mother took a deep breath, laying a hand on Kacey's shoulder. "You won't have to fight anyone until you're 18, or unless the new Kaderian wearer is chosen," Ciara's eyes grew serious, "You'll have to protect them, Kacey because if anyone gets the antigen of the Kaderian, it'll be over for the wearer."

Kacey's brow furrowed, and her mind raced with questions. "What's the opposite of the Kaderian?" she asked, a hint of curiosity in her voice.

"The Bradaetha," Ciara replied, her voice hushed as if the name itself carried an ancient weight. "Come with me."

She led Kacey to a small, hidden room in the house that she had never seen before. The room smelled of old wood and history, and the walls were lined with books and artifacts. Ciara picked up an ancient scroll, unrolling it with careful hands.

"Many years ago, there was a peaceful community called Kadut," Ciara began, "They were hardworking and friendly. Eventually, the people of Kadut decided to create a cloth to protect them in case of war. It was the Kaderian cloth. It gave its wearer four great powers: invisibility, illusion, indestructibility, and teleportation. Not just the ability to move to known places, but even to unknown ones."

Kacey's eyes widened as she listened. She was intrigued despite her fear.

"But," Ciara continued, her tone darkening, "There was another community – the Bradea. Their king wanted all the power in the world, and he started a war to claim it. That's when the Kaderian cloth was first used. It was so powerful, but it became uncontrollable. The wearer was consumed by it."

Ciara's voice became even quieter, "After the Bradean king was killed, the people of Kadut and Bradea realized the Kaderian could not be controlled. They forged the Bradaetha, which was a counterpart cloth to control the Kaderian and keep its power in check. And that's where your father's lineage comes in."

Kacey was silent, taking in the gravity of her mother's words. "But how am I supposed to guide the Kaderian user if I don't have any powers?" she asked.

Ciara smiled softly, shaking her head when she said, "You don't need powers, Kacey. The truth is, none of the Kaderian's abilities can affect you. You're immune to them." She paused, then added, "Oh, and I almost forgot! The Barro also has advanced speed. But don't use it too often. It drains you."

Kacey's mind was spinning as she tried to process everything. She was destined to be the Barro, a protector of the Kaderian wearer, someone who could stand against its immense power. But she was just a girl, and this was a legacy she hadn't asked for.

Ciara walked over to a corner of the room, where a small training area had been set up. "We'll start training now," she said gently, "I'll teach you everything your father knew."

Kacey swallowed hard, her hands still gripping the bow and arrow her mother had given her. She wasn't ready for this. Not at all. But as she looked into her mother's eyes, full of hope and sadness, she knew there was no turning back.

This was her fate.

Chapter 11

As Kacey trained under her mother's watchful eye, she grew more confident with each passing day. Her muscles strengthened, her reflexes sharpened, and the bow and arrow she once feared became like an extension of herself. The weight of her responsibility as the Barro still lingered, but she had started to feel like she could handle it. That is, until the day of the showcasing of the new Kaderian user.

It happened at school, in the middle of an ordinary afternoon. Kacey had been sitting on the floor in a corner of the hall, trying to stay unnoticed when the Army arrived. Everyone's attention was instantly drawn to the uniformed soldiers who walked in, their presence commanding the room. Then, the previous Kaderian wearer followed. It was a woman whose age had begun to show, the burden of the cloth too much for her to bear any longer. She was there to transfer the Kaderian cloth to its next user.

The room buzzed with excitement, but all Kacey could feel was dread. She knew what was coming. And she knew she would have to protect whoever was chosen.

Later that evening, Kacey stormed into the house, slamming the door behind her. "Mum, there's no way I can protect the Kaderian user!" she cried, dropping her bag on the floor.

Ciara, seated calmly in the living room, didn't even flinch. Instead, she calmly asked, "What happened to your oath, Kacey?"

Kacey's frustration bubbled over. "It's not that! It's a boy! I don't want him falling in love with me! Boys are stupid! They always do dumb things, and now one of them is going to have *this* kind of power!"

Ciara raised an eyebrow, "Well, then guide him."

"But Mum-"

"No buts," Ciara interrupted firmly, "End of discussion. You have a duty to serve, and you must do it." She rose from her chair and left the room without another word.

Kacey stood there, fists clenched, her mind racing. "Now what do I do? There's no way he won't mess up with the power... or fail the missions," she muttered to herself. Then, an idea sparked in her mind. "Oh, I know. I can help him."

With renewed determination, Kacey headed to her room, preparing for the next step in her journey as the Barro.

*********END OF FLASHBACK*********

"And that's why I'm here," Barro – Kacey – finished, her voice soft but steady as she looked at Jark.

Jark's brow furrowed in confusion. "Wait... are you not Tabitha?"

Kacey nodded, a small, almost sad smile on her lips. "Yes, I'm also Tabitha."

Jark took a moment to process this, his mind spinning with all the revelations. "What else do you know about me?" he asked, his voice harsher now, demanding answers.

Kacey hesitated, glancing down for a moment before meeting his eyes again, "Well, apart from realizing you didn't want to be the Kaderian wearer... I had a chance to stop them, but-"

"You what?" Jark interrupted, his voice rising in disbelief.

Kacey's eyes filled with regret as she said, "I had a chance to stop them from choosing you. But if I did, then there would be no one else to wear it," she admitted quietly.

Jark's face twisted in anger, "So, you made them ruin my already miserable life just so I could become a killer? Like I don't have a choice?!" He stood, fists clenched, glaring at her. "I'm not even sure your name is really Tabitha, or Kacey, or whoever you are," he added, his voice shaking with fury. Tabitha was the girl in his college, the one his friends had teased him about. Now, here she was, telling him how she had known, how she could have stopped them, but she hadn't done it, or been able to do it.

Jark didn't know how to feel about it all.

"They're both my names," Kacey continued, her tone firm but apologetic, "I wanted it to be like I had two different identities. One as Barro and one as me."

Jark's rage boiled over at her words, and in that moment of rage, he reached for his sword, almost ready to lash out. His hand gripped the hilt tightly, and Kacey could see the internal struggle in his eyes. But just as quickly, Jark stopped himself, taking a deep breath as he tried to cool down.

"I can't believe this. No, I just *can't*," Jark spat, his voice dripping with bitterness. "I was taken away, forced to live this miserable life, and all because you needed a hero. Well, newsflash! I'm not a hero. I wish I could drop this damn hoodie, but I can't. So, goodbye." His words were sharp and final, each one cutting like a blade.

He turned on his heel and stormed toward the door, leaving Kacey standing there, her heart sinking.

"But this is your home," she called after him, her voice laced with desperation. She didn't want him to leave like this, not with so much unresolved between them.

Jark paused for a moment at the door, glancing back at her. His eyes were hollow, filled with the weight of too much pain, too much betrayal. Without saying another word, he continued walking out, letting the door swing shut behind him.

Kacey stood there in the silence that followed, feeling a knot of guilt tighten in her chest. She had tried to help him, tried to guide him, but now it felt like she had only made things worse. What had she expected? That Jark would just accept everything she had said? That he would somehow forgive her for the role she played in his suffering? She sighed, knowing the road ahead wouldn't be easy for either of them.

***

Jark's feet carried him away from the house, but his mind was still stuck on everything Kacey had told him. He didn't want to believe it. He couldn't. How could she have let them ruin his life like that, knowing what it would do to him? Anger still simmered in his chest, but there was also a growing sense of despair.

He didn't know where he was going, but after what felt like hours of wandering, he found himself at a bar. The neon lights flickered in the dim evening light, and he could hear the low murmur of voices from inside. It was a familiar place, one of the few places he had come to drown out the voice of the hoodie when it became too much.

Jark pushed open the door and walked in, the scent of alcohol and cigarette smoke hitting him immediately. The bar was dimly lit, and a few patrons scattered around the room lost in their own thoughts and drinks. He made his way to the counter and sat down, wondering how he could escape these thoughts without indulging in alcohol.

Chapter 12

San had replayed that day in his head a thousand times. The day he lost both his best friends.

It had started out normal, like any other day. He met up with Jark in the college corridors and together they went to look for Kadrea.

It was exactly what they did every morning. The three of them were inseparable – a unit. They'd known each other since freshman year, a bond forged through late-night study sessions shared meals, and a common dislike for their physics professor. On that day, he never imagined how quickly everything would fall apart.

When Jark pulled Kadrea aside, San didn't think anything of it. Maybe Jark had something personal to discuss with him. He trusted them and didn't need to pry into every conversation. So, San waved them off, saying he'd meet them later at the café.

But that never happened.

Later that day, the news spread like wildfire: Kadrea was dead. Found at the back of the school, his body abandoned behind the gym, throat slit. Everyone was talking about the Hoodie Assassin. The same killer who'd been responsible for a string of brutal murders in the city. And worse, Jark was nowhere to be found.

San hadn't believed the rumors at first. Jark was his friend. No way he'd kill Kadrea, no matter what the police and the media were saying. The Hoodie Assassin had been on the loose for months, leaving a trail of bodies in the shadows of the city, but they hadn't been connected to any real person. The idea that Jark, of all people, could be tied to that was absurd.

He'd gone straight to Jark's house that evening, pounding on the door until his fists were raw. But Jark's parents turned him away. "He's locked himself in his room," they'd said, eyes hollow, voices distant. "He's not seeing anyone."

San had never felt so helpless, standing there on their doorstep, unsure of what to do next. Jark was his best friend. Kadrea was dead, and now Jark had vanished from his life, too.

The next day, things got worse.

He had been leaving the college, still numb from the news of Kadrea's death, when he saw it – saw him. Jark, standing on the roof of the main building. San froze, a cold wave of dread washing over him. He shouted and sprinted towards the building, but he was too far away. Jark was just a silhouette against the sky. And then, in a single heartbeat, his best friend was falling.

San reached him just as the paramedics arrived. But it didn't matter Jark was already gone.

Everything had changed that day. Kadrea gone. Jark gone. And all that was left was the burning question of why. Why had

Kadrea died? Why had Jark jumped? The media had fed the frenzy with rumors that Jark had been the Hoodie Assassin all along, but San never bought it. Jark wasn't capable of something like that. He was sure of it.

From that day forward, San had made a promise to himself. He was going to find the real Hoodie Assassin. He was going to uncover the truth. Maybe then, the guilt that had been gnawing at him for five years would finally loosen its grip. Maybe he'd be able to make peace with the fact that he hadn't been there when it mattered most, that he hadn't seen the signs.

Five years. Five long years, and still, San hadn't made much progress. The Hoodie Assassin had disappeared not long after Jark's death, the trail going cold. The police had all but given up, moving on to other cases. But not San. He held on, searching for any thread of information that could lead him to the truth.

He found no one to help him though, because most of the people, and even the police believed that Jark was the Hoodie Assassin, and he was dead. Hence, they didn't need to work that hard on a case that was already pretty obvious.

San tried to find something, any kind of clue, but the trail had gone silent. Sometimes, San wondered if he was chasing ghosts.

The bar he worked at was quiet that evening. He'd taken the job not long after he gave up on finishing his degree. The whole "future" thing had seemed pointless after everything that had happened. So, he worked nights at the bar, kept his head down, and tried not to think too hard about the past.

That night, as San was wiping down the counter, something about the room shifted. He felt it before he saw it. A prickle on the back of his neck. The sensation that he was being watched.

And then, the door creaked open. He looked up, and his world flipped upside down.

Jark.

San's breath caught in his throat. Standing at the entrance, in the dim light of the bar, was the man he'd watched die five years ago. The man who had disappeared from his life left a trail of destruction and shattered everything San had believed in.

He blinked, half-expecting the vision to vanish. But Jark didn't move, didn't waver. He was real. Somehow, impossibly, standing right there in front of him.

San's hands shook as he set the cloth down, taking an unsteady step forward, but his words died on his lips.

How was his best friend here when he should be dead?

He watched in shock as Jark slowly walked towards the bar counter and sat himself on one of the stools.

San didn't move because to him it felt like Jark was an apparition and that he would vanish the moment San so much as breathed.

But Jark didn't disappear. He sat there, staring at the counter top glumly, lost in his own thoughts.

So San gathered his wits and thoughts and finally approached him. He watched Jark closely and once he felt like the staring was going to turn into gawking, San cleared his throat lightly and finally asked Jark to tell him what he wanted to drink.

But the real questions he wanted to ask went so much deeper than that.

Chapter 13

Jark stepped into the bar, the weight of the hoodie heavy on his shoulders, both literally and metaphorically. He had spent the last few years in the shadows, unseen and unnoticed, and the air inside felt different – almost foreign. It was quieter than most bars he had been in, the dim light casting long shadows over the small tables scattered around the room. It was exactly what he needed. Somewhere to disappear for a while, to think.

The bartender was polishing glasses, standing to the side, but he paused in his ministrations when Jark entered.

Whatever, Jark didn't have enough time to see what everyone else in the room was up to.

Jark slid into one of the seats at the bar and stared at the countertop for a moment, looking down but not really seeing anything. He was lost in thoughts about all that had happened with him and to him in the past years.

"What can I get you?" came the bartender's voice, feeling like he was trying to choke his words out.

Jark sighed lowly. His throat felt dry, but alcohol wasn't going to help. He needed his mind clear. "I'll just have a glass of water," he said at last.

The bartender raised an eyebrow, seeming to gain his confidence, and saying, "Just water? We've got the finest wines, beer, whatever you'd like."

"I don't drink," Jark replied, his voice low, "And I'm…really upset."

The bartender gave him an appraising look, setting down the glass in his hand. "Normally, people I meet drink or smoke their problems away. How come you don't?"

Jark shrugged, offering a half-smile, "At a young age, I admired Samson. You know, from the Bible. He got his strength from his hair, and he never drank. I figured if it worked for him, maybe it would for me too."

The bartender seemed to think over his words for a moment before he chuckled lightly, "You know it wasn't the hair, right? God gave him that strength."

Jark nodded, "Yeah, I know. But for me, it's about control. Keeping myself from doing something that might hurt my body. Addiction is a dangerous thing."

The bartender's smile faded as he set the glass of water in front of Jark and said, "Fair enough. Though, not sure why you're telling me all this."

Jark's face tightened, realizing how much he had already shared. "I didn't come here to explain my drinking habits. Not really your business, is it?" he said with a bite to his voice. It didn't mean anything. Jark had developed his snarkiness as a defense mechanism.

The bartender raised his hands, palms out, in a gesture of surrender, "Sorry. You just reminded me of an old friend I had back in college."

Jark froze. The air seemed to shift between them. He didn't know why, but something about the bartender's words tugged at a buried memory. "He must've been a better guy than me," Jark muttered. "Unlike me, the traitor…I can't even believe I killed my friend." The words slipped out before Jark could stop them, and his eyes widened with realization. Then he scrambled, "Wait – no, that's not true. I was…just joking. Never mind."

But the damage was done. The bartender's expression didn't change much, but Jark could sense a tension in the air now.

The bartender paused for a moment, then said quietly, "How are things, Jark?"

Jark's heart skipped a beat. He hadn't told anyone his name. His fingers tensed around the glass of water. "How did you know my name?"

Silence. The bartender glanced up, meeting Jark's eyes.

And suddenly, it clicked.

"You're Kadrea," Jark said, half hoping, half fearing it was true. Maybe this was some twisted reality where he hadn't died after all.

But the bartender shook his head, and Jark felt a small relief wash over him. But then…who was he?

"Then who are you…" Jark's mind scrambled for names, trying to make sense of it all. "Jacky, Sango, Hecu…Baru, Preda…"

"Stop," the bartender interrupted, his voice firm but calm, "I'm Sanja."

San. The realization hit Jark like a punch to the gut. "I was getting there," Jark tried to joke, though his voice wavered.

"No, you weren't," San shot back, a smirk pulling at the corner of his mouth.

"Yes, I was," Jark insisted, though he knew he wasn't fooling anyone.

"No, you weren't."

They continued bickering like that for a moment, the absurdity of the situation making Jark feel more alive than he had in years. This was San, his old friend, someone he thought he'd never see again.

"Okay, fine, I wasn't," Jark finally conceded, rolling his eyes. "You happy now?"

"Yeah," San replied, his grin widening, "Yeah, I am."

The brief levity quickly faded, though, as the weight of their past returned to the surface. "So, how's life as an assassin?" San asked, his tone only half-joking. "It must be cool, right? Wait – how did you not die? That fall was massive."

Jark glanced around the bar, making sure no one else was close enough to hear. He leaned in slightly to say, "I could tell you…but not here. Too many people. I don't want anyone to know my identity."

San nodded, the playful spark in his eyes dimming. "Right. Sorry."

"You don't need to apologize," Jark said, his voice softening. "I'm the one who owes you an apology. For everything."

San studied him for a moment, the tension between them growing thicker.

Feeling like he was being studied too closely, Jark blurted out, "Was Tabitha there? When…you know."

San blinked, surprised by the question, and shook his head, "Honestly, I don't know."

Jark's brow furrowed. "That's… sad."

"How's that sad?" San asked, confused.

Jark shook his head, "Never mind."

Jark leaned back in his seat, looking San up and down. "What about you? Why are you working in a place like this? What happened to you?"

San exhaled slowly, rubbing the back of his neck before saying, "It's a long story. After college, I scored high enough to try for a scholarship. I got it, but my parents weren't too thrilled about me doing all that without telling them. So, they cut me off. Now, I work here at night and go to school during the day."

"That must be exhausting," Jark said, feeling a pang of guilt. San had been dealing with all of this on his own, while Jark had been consumed by his own darkness.

"Yeah, it's pretty rough," San admitted. "I haven't had a proper meal in a year."

Jark's jaw tightened, "Hey, don't worry about that. I can help. But you might have to close for the night."

San's eyes widened slightly, "You serious?"

"Yeah," Jark said. "Go tell your manager."

San stood there for a moment, staring at Jark like he was seeing a ghost – which, in a way, he was. But then, without another word, he turned and made his way to the back of the bar.

Jark watched him go, the familiar ache of guilt gnawing at his chest. He had survived, somehow, but he hadn't really lived. Not like San had. He wasn't sure if he deserved a second chance, but for the first time in years, he felt like maybe, just maybe, he wasn't completely alone.

Chapter 14

Jark waits for San to come back for the next five minutes. He still feels shock reverberating through his body at the thought that he found someone he used to know in college. That time feels like a lifetime ago even though it had been only five years.

So much changed in so little time and now Jark feels like his life before becoming the Hoodie Assassin was not his life but someone else's entirely.

His thoughts halt when San walks back over, his face painted with a heavy expression, like he's carrying something he's trying to keep hidden. Jark could tell by the way San's shoulders slumped.

"What did he say?" Jark asked, trying to ease him into the conversation. His heart raced a little, though, knowing San was trying to make it a moment. San always liked to mess with him.

"He said... I can... not..." San said, dragging out each word as if savoring the drama.

"Please, just say yes or no, man," Jark blurted out, frustration edging his voice. He hated when people beat around the bush.

San sighed, shaking his head before saying, "He said I cannot keep working hard and not eating properly."

Relief flooded through Jark, and he let out a breath. "So, it's a yes, let's go then," he said, turning to leave before San could play any more mind games.

But, of course, San pulled him back, "Hold on, why are you going in that direction?"

"We're walking, obviously," Jark said, giving him a look that said it was the most normal thing in the world. "I don't trust anyone."

"Not even your own friend?" San asked, a trace of hurt in his voice. He always was the more sentimental one between the three of them.

"Well..." Jark started, but before he could explain himself, San grabbed his arm and dragged him toward the parking lot.

"What the-?" Jark stopped mid-sentence, staring at the car in front of them. It was a sleek, almost futuristic-looking vehicle. "You have a car?" he asked San, dumbfounded.

"Yeah, I do. Although…" San replied casually like it was no big deal.

"Although what? You have a car that looks new, actually, it looks exactly like the recent one with adverts everywhere! Jark tried hard to think about the name of the car but his memory these days was no good. He sighed, "Never mind, it doesn't matter what type of car it is, what matters is that you have a car!"

San chuckled, then said with just a hint of pride, "Although I made it myself."

"No way, that is super cool," Jark said, genuinely impressed as they climbed inside. The seats were comfortable, and the car smelled new, like leather and fresh paint. San was always full of surprises.

The car hummed to life as they pulled out of the parking lot. At first, the silence between them was comfortable. Years of unspoken things lay between them, and Jark didn't know where to start, so he focused on the road.

After what felt like hours, Jark glanced over at him and asked, "Dude, where are you going?"

San glanced at him with a sheepish grin, "I have no idea. You're supposed to lead me."

Jark raised an eyebrow, "But you're not even paying attention."

"The map knows the route," San shrugged, tapping the dashboard. "See? We're almost there."

He was right. Somehow, they'd made it to the restaurant. Jark shook his head, laughing softly, "Yeah, whatever. Let's just go eat."

Inside, it was warm and smelled like fried food and spices, the kind of place that always felt like home no matter how much you'd changed. They found a table and settled in.

Immediately, a waitress approached with a warm smile and asked, "What would you like?"

They ordered, but the moment she walked away, San turned to Jark, the casual air slipping away.

"How was college without us?" Jark asked, trying to fill the silence, but also genuinely curious.

San looked down at the table, his fingers tracing the edge of the napkin as he replied, "At first, I was popular. Then it became a misery. Everyone didn't want to be with me because anyone I was with...surprisingly died."

Jark froze, the weight of San's words sinking in. "That sounds awful," he said, though he knew there was more.

"Yeah, it is. And all of them always have a claw mark on their chest," San added, his voice dropping lower.

Jark blinked, his mind racing. "Hmmm... that sounds familiar," he murmured, though he already knew where this was going.

San looked up at him, eyes searching his face for answers. "What made you become a killer?" he asked suddenly. There it was. The question that had been hanging between them since Jark walked into the bar. The question he'd been avoiding his whole life.

Jark looked down at his hands, his fingers curling into fists. "I was forced," he said, his voice quieter than he intended. The memories flooded back. The blood, fear, and the crushing sense of helplessness. "And surprisingly, Tabitha was part of it."

San's eyes widened and he gasped, "No way. How did you know?"

Jark let out a long breath, leaning back in his seat. "It's just... what I feel," he said, but the truth was more complicated than that. Jark could not tell San everything even though were old friends. It was too much for a person to take in and it would take hours for San to understand.

It was better this way.

Before San could press for more, the waitress came back with their food, and the smell of it pulled Jark back to the present. He picked up his fork, trying to push away the darkness creeping around the edges of his thoughts. But it was hard to shake the feeling that no matter how much he tried to leave it behind, the past kept dragging him back.

They ate in silence for a while, both lost in their own thoughts. The food was good, better than Jark had expected, but it felt like there was a wall between them now. He looked over at San, wondering if he was thinking the same thing, about how they used to be before everything went wrong. Before the hoodie, before Kadrea, before Jark became something he didn't recognize in the mirror.

"You know," Jark finally said, breaking the silence, "I didn't choose this. Any of it."

San didn't say anything at first, just looked at him with that same sad expression he'd been wearing since the moment they started talking.

"I know," San said eventually. "But it doesn't change what's happened."

Jark nodded, swallowing hard. The truth was, he didn't know if he could ever make it right.

Chapter 15

At the back of the dimly lit bar, Danse sat in a chair, his gaze sharp and unwavering. Flanked by two men, one of whom held a briefcase, he felt the tension in the air. Across from him, a man lounged casually in his seat, a smirk on his lips, and several armed guards by his side. They were all waiting, watching, the weight of the moment bearing down on them.

Danse broke the silence. "We're here with the money. We need the information," he said, his voice steady, as Gera, his trusted partner, stepped forward with the briefcase.

The man in the chair chuckled, an arrogant sound that grated on Danse's nerves. "Oh, nice. I like your determination," the man said slowly, leaning back as if they had all the time in the world. "But you do realize the village is heavily guarded? Ancient weapons, things you've probably never seen before."

Danse's patience was wearing thin. "How does that help us?" he snapped, his eyes narrowing. "We have a plan. All you need to do is provide the information. That's what we're paying you for, isn't it?"

At that, the men beside the seated man raised their weapons, tension crackling in the air. But the man gave a small signal with his hand, and they held their fire.

"How interesting," the man said with a sly grin, "You've got the guts of a real man. But I think I'll need an additional three million for your…disrespect."

Danse clenched his fists, his frustration boiling, but before he could respond, Gera cut in.

"Okay, fine," Gera said calmly, reaching for a second briefcase. The man on the seat raised an eyebrow in surprise, clearly not expecting Gera to have anticipated the demand.

Danse turned to Gera, frowning, "What is that for?"

Gera glanced at him, a small smile tugging at his lips. "Well, I knew you'd want to cause a scene, and I figured they'd want extra money. I didn't want you to die over it. I love you too much for that to happen."

Danse's frustration softened for a moment. "Fine. Give it to them. We have a world to conquer," he said, gesturing toward the briefcase.

The exchange was quick. The men on the other side eagerly took the second briefcase and inspected it as Danse and Gera made their way out. The man in the chair, now satisfied, waved them off.

As they left, the man in the chair opened the briefcases. His smug grin disappeared when he realized the second briefcase was filled with fake money. He slammed it shut, laughing bitterly. "These men think I'm a child," he muttered.

Back at their hideout, Danse and Gera opened their own briefcase. Inside, the papers were burned, the edges curled and charred. Suddenly, a hologram flickered to life, the image of their contact grinning smugly. "Did you think I wasn't two steps ahead of you?" the voice taunted.

Danse scoffed, leaning back. "And we are three steps ahead of you," he said confidently, as Gera retrieved a small device. He activated it, revealing a reintegration mechanism they had prepared for this very situation.

*********One Hour Later*********

Danse groaned, pacing the room. "Why is this taking so long?"

Gera, seated at a computer, didn't look up. "Like I told you before, but you never listen – this is just a test. It's not confirmed to work yet," he said, sounding exasperated.

A soft bell rang from the machine, and Gera finally turned to face him. "It's done."

"Finally," Danse said, rushing over to the computer. He picked up the map displayed on the screen. His brow furrowed. "The map is broken," he grumbled, squinting at the disoriented lines and coordinates.

Gera sighed and gently rotated the map. "It's upside down," he corrected. "What would you do without me?"

Danse shot him a look, half amused, half annoyed, "I'm going to pretend like I didn't hear that and focus on what I'm doing."

He scrutinized the map closely, matching the markings with locations on Earth. His fingers traced a path as he muttered under his breath, working through the puzzle. Gera leaned over, watching him work.

"The city is located close to a country called Nigeria, in a place known as Delta State," the computer announced, its monotone voice cutting through the room.

Danse straightened up, satisfaction flickering across his face. "Now we know the location. Tomorrow, we set out," he said, his voice full of determination.

The tension that had hung over the room seemed to dissipate slightly, though both men knew this was just the beginning. The village they were after was rumored to be more than just heavily guarded – it was nearly impenetrable. Ancient weapons, powerful guardians, and secrets that had been locked away for centuries.

Danse had no illusions about the challenges ahead. The journey to Nigeria would be treacherous, and even if they reached the village, getting what they came for would be another battle entirely. But they were prepared for this. He and Gera had been planning for months, gathering resources, and outwitting their enemies at every turn.

He glanced over at Gera, who was packing up the equipment, methodical as always. Danse felt a surge of gratitude for his partner. Gera wasn't just his backup – he was the reason they had made it this far without getting themselves killed. He was the one who always thought two steps ahead, the one who balanced Danse's recklessness with logic and reason.

"You think we're really ready for this?" Gera asked, his voice quieter now, the gravity of the mission settling in.

Danse didn't hesitate. "We're ready. We've come too far to turn back now."

Gera nodded but didn't say anything else. They both knew what was at stake – power, fortune, and survival. But for Danse, it was more than that. It was about proving something, about taking control of his own fate. No one was going to tell him what he could or couldn't do, and no village, no matter how ancient or well-guarded, was going to stand in his way.

As the night deepened and the world outside their hideout grew quiet, Danse felt the weight of the coming days pressing down on him. Tomorrow, they would step into the unknown, but that was where he thrived.

Chapter 16

On the ride to Jark's place, the conversation started off light-heartedly as San grumbled about his apartment situation. "I'm just going to drop you off and head home. I just hope no one wrecked it again," San sighed. "For the past year, it's been a mess, and my landlord's threatening to send me packing."

Jark glanced over, giving his friend a sympathetic look. "You know, you could crash at my place if you want," he offered.

San's response was immediate. "Thanks, but nooooooooooooway," he laughed as they approached a large, modern-looking house. His laughter turned to disbelief when he realized they were pulling up to Jark's address. "Wait, is this…your house?" San asked, eyebrows shooting up.

"Yeah," Jark replied nonchalantly.

"How are you affording something this big?" San asked in amazement.

Jark shrugged. "I'll take any job that involves killing, whether it's for the government or anyone willing to pay. Nearly got caught a few times, but this power helps a lot," he said, then vanished in front of San.

San blinked, looking around wildly. "Where'd you go?" he asked.

"Right here," Jark said, reappearing with a slight smirk.

San chuckled, visibly relieved, "Cool. Glad I don't have to be the one doing that kind of work."

"Why's that?" Jark asked, genuinely curious.

"Because I'd get caught in seconds," San admitted, and they both laughed as they exited the car and walked up to the door.

"Watch this," Jark said with a grin, standing in front of the entrance. "Open for Jarkor Danga."

San raised an eyebrow. "How would that even work? It's not-" Before he could finish, the door opened wide enough for them and the car to slide in.

As the car moved forward on its own, San's eyes widened. "How are we moving? And how's the car moving by itself?" he exclaimed, looking around as if the house might respond.

Jark smirked, "I'm surprised a 'genius' like you wouldn't recognize a technological house."

"Oh, I knew that," San lied quickly as they stepped into the sitting room, taking in the enormous space.

"Wow, this place is huge!" San said, his awe turning into disbelief when he spotted someone standing near the far wall.

Jark seemed to have forgotten that Kacey was there. "Oh…right. Forgot you were here," he muttered, sighing.

San's gaze darted between them, sensing the tension, "Who's this?"

"Just some girl who broke into my house," Jark muttered.

"I saved your life, you idiot!" Kacey snapped back.

"After ruining it," Jark replied dryly.

"Well, it sounds like there's some marriage drama here, so I'll just…be in the kitchen," San said, edging away.

"Sanja, sit down and don't go anywhere," Jark commanded.

Kacey crossed her arms. "Oh, so now you're giving orders? What's next, Mr. 'My Life is Ruined'?" she retorted.

"This might be even better with some popcorn…Are you two even dating?" San teased, sinking back into the couch.

"No," Jark replied flatly.

An hour later, San was munching on actual popcorn, watching the two of them bicker. "When did you even get popcorn?" Jark asked, a little exasperated.

San shrugged and said, "While you two were busy arguing."

Kacey rolled her eyes. "We were not arguing," she insisted.

San chuckled. "Seemed like it to me," he said, then stood up, stretching. "Well, I'm going to my room if anyone needs me," he announced, heading for the guest room.

"Same here. And I don't expect anyone – especially Kacey or Tabitha – to need me," Jark said, disappearing down the hall to his own room.

Hours later, the house was quiet as everyone slept, until a loud bang from the kitchen shattered the silence. Kacey bolted upright in bed, rubbing her eyes and trying to wake up. "What could that be?" she mumbled, padding toward the noise.

In the hallway, Jark stood transfixed, eyes glazed as he watched a girl – one who wasn't really there. "Oh, it's you again," he murmured, staring at the mysterious figure he knew as Echo.

"Oh, it's you again," Echo repeated, mimicking his words in a taunting tone.

"Why do you always do that? Just…answer me!" Jark snapped, his voice filled with frustration. "What are you? Who are you?" But instead of replying, she turned and walked away, and he followed, almost hypnotized.

Meanwhile, Kacey shook San awake, explaining Jark's odd behavior. "He's…sleepwalking or something," she whispered as they tried to catch up with him.

Jark continued to follow Echo through a surreal, dreamlike landscape that wasn't part of the house anymore. He could see lush flowers blooming in every color and trees that shimmered with otherworldly hues. "Where are we?" he asked, but as soon as he reached for her, the Echo, she turned to him, and they kissed. But the scene suddenly dissolved as water splashed over his face.

Jark snapped back to reality, sputtering. "Hey! What was that for?" he demanded, wiping his face.

"Trust me, you don't want to know," Kacey said, clearly amused. San was by the sink, frantically rinsing his mouth, looking both embarrassed and horrified.

Jark blinked, bewildered, "What's going on here?"

"That's what we're asking you," Kacey replied, folding her arms. San took a seat on the far end of the couch, muttering to himself, "First, he wanted to kill me, then he kissed me…what's become of me…what am I doing with my life?"

Kacey raised an eyebrow, "You were dreaming, I think, or rather, sleepwalking. What exactly happened, Jark?"

"I had this dream, and I saw this girl – not you by the way she is way finer than you," Jark explained, but his voice trailed off as he noticed Kacey's deadpan stare.

"Trust me, we got the picture," she retorted. "In our version, you basically tried to kill San and then kissed him."

Jark's face twisted in disgust. "No…no way!"

Kacey sighed. "You might want to talk to him. I'm going back to bed," she said, walking away.

Jark reluctantly sat beside San, who looked more distressed than ever. "Listen, San, I know what happened was…a misunderstanding."

San stopped him, holding up a hand. "A misunderstanding? Jark, that was beyond awkward. It was…I don't even know what to say."

San stood up, shaking his head. "I'm done. I'm leaving," he said, stomping up the stairs. "I can't believe that just happened," he muttered.

"But…" Jark started, but San's door slammed shut behind him.

Left alone, Jark sighed. "He'll come around…eventually."

Suddenly, the room grew darker, and an eerie chill filled the air. "Who's there?" Jark called, his voice tense.

A familiar voice answered, dripping with malice. "I am your worst nightmare," Kadrea's voice hissed from the shadows.

Jark clasped his hands over his ears, backing away. "But I…I said I was sorry for killing you! What else do you want from me?" he cried out, his voice filled with despair. "Why does my life keep getting worse?"

"Because you made it that way," Kadrea's voice answered, the words slicing through the silence like knives.

Without thinking, Jark turned and bolted, crashing through a window to escape. Shards of glass scattered around him as he hit the ground outside, panting and looking around, but the dark presence was gone.

Inside, Kacey and San stirred at the noise. Kacey poked her head out of her door, groggy and confused. "Did he just…jump out the window?"

San sighed, rubbing his eyes. "Typical Jark."

Chapter 17

After thirteen long hours in the air, Danse and Gera finally touched down in Nigeria, weary but alert as they navigated through the bustling airport.

"Welcome to Nigeria," Danse said, a slight smile tugging at his lips.

Gera glanced around, visibly impressed. "This place is even more beautiful up close," Gera murmured as they made their way outside and quickly flagged down a taxi.

"It's 2000 naira to your destination," the driver announced, eyeing them expectantly.

Danse and Gera exchanged a glance. "Uh...we only have dollars," Gera admitted, glancing at the driver with an apologetic shrug.

The driver sighed, then gestured off to the side, "There's a shop nearby where you can exchange dollars for naira."

Danse's patience snapped. They'd traveled far, and every second lost was valuable. He stepped forward, his tone sharp. "Give us a ride to the national airport," he said, his voice carrying a threat, "or I'll make you regret it."

The driver raised an eyebrow, unfazed. "Abeg, what other suffer you wan to bring? You no know say this country na hell on its own? Either you pay, or forget about it," he replied, lapsing into Nigerian Pidgin English.

Danse felt a flicker of frustration, but Gera stepped forward, hands raised in a calming gesture. "Please, just help us out."

The driver let out a sigh, finally relenting. "Alright, alright. I also accept dollars."

Gera brightened, pulling a bill from the bag, "How about $20 for the ride?"

The driver laughed. "My friend, make it $200, and we've got a deal."

Gera hesitated but nodded, and they shook on it. As they slid into the back seat, Danse felt the tension ease a bit, though his eyes remained fixed on the road.

After what felt like hours, Danse leaned forward. "How long will this take?"

The driver looked at him in the mirror, a bit amused. "Brother, just dey calm down nah," he said. "Me be driver; when we get there, we get there."

Danse settled back, exhaling as he glanced out the window at the vibrant streets passing by, filled with sights and sounds unfamiliar yet captivating.

***

Jark sat at the edge of the lake, his gaze fixed on the calm water that rippled under a light breeze. He sighed, frustration evident in the tight line of his jaw.

"Why does everything in my life have to be such a mess?" he muttered, watching his reflection shift with each ripple.

A voice behind him broke his solitude. "I get that," San said softly.

Jark turned, surprised to see him standing there. "San? I thought you left."

San shifted awkwardly, hands in his pockets, glancing off to the side. "Yeah, about that…Look, I know what happened back there was awkward – more than awkward, really – but I thought, maybe, I should find out if it's real. Or, at least, if there's any truth to it."

Jark frowned, confused. "If what is true?"

San hesitated, his gaze holding a mixture of vulnerability and bravery. "Do you…like me?" he asked, his voice quiet but firm.

Jark blinked, caught off guard by the question. He chuckled, shaking his head. "No offense, San, but no. I don't really believe in love anymore – not since everything happened with Tabitha, or was it Kacey?"

San visibly relaxed, a slight smile forming. "Oh, that's actually a relief," he cleared his throat, looking away, "My old house was sold while I was gone. They figured I wasn't coming back, I guess, and I was behind on payments anyway."

"Really?" Jark said, genuinely surprised. "That's... rough. I wanted to see the place, just out of curiosity."

San's brow furrowed, confused. "Wait, what do you mean by 'wanted to see it'?"

Jark allowed himself a small grin. "Well, since you're asking, I was the one who bought it. Last night, actually."

San's eyes widened in disbelief. "No way! You actually bought it?"

"Yeah." Jark rubbed the back of his neck. "I figured it might be good for you to have a place again. Besides, I thought you'd probably hate me after...well, you know."

San stared at him for a moment, then lunged forward, wrapping Jark in an impulsive hug. "Thank you, man. Seriously, thank you."

Jark froze, patting San's back stiffly, "Okay, easy, buddy. Remember, the hoodie still has a mind of its own."

San pulled back quickly, an embarrassed grin on his face. "Sorry, I just...I'm just really happy."

A smirk tugged at Jark's lips, "How about we go somewhere else?"

San shrugged, nodding. "Yeah, no problem. Where to?"

Jark led him along a wooded trail, winding through the trees until they emerged in a hidden clearing. Sunlight filtered through the dense canopy above, dappling the ground in patches of light. A hush fell over the space, and a gentle breeze rustled the leaves.

"This is where I come when…you know when things get out of control," Jark admitted, gesturing around the tranquil spot.

San's gaze roamed over the clearing, admiration, and wonder in his eyes. "This place is incredible. It's so…peaceful."

Jark nodded, looking up at the trees and breathing in the clean air. "It's the only place where I can really think, where the hoodie feels…quieter."

San sat down on a fallen log, his usual energy subdued in the calm atmosphere, "I can see why. It's like this place is hidden away from everything else, like a little world of its own."

Jark joined him, staring out into the trees as he said, "When things get bad, it's good to remember there's something outside of all that chaos. Even if it's just for a few minutes."

They fell into a companionable silence, each lost in their own thoughts. The lake shimmered through the trees in the distance, and for a moment, Jark felt like he was free from everything – the hoodie, the past, the guilt.

San broke the silence, his voice soft, "You know, whatever happens, you've got this. And if you ever need someone to remind you of that…well, you've got me."

Jark gave him a faint smile, nodding. "Thanks, San." For the first time in a long while, he felt the weight on his shoulders lift, even if only for a fleeting moment.

Chapter 18

The air inside the abandoned warehouse was thick with dust and the stale scent of disuse. Claw Fist's heavy steps echoed as he approached the center of the large, empty space, his eyes narrowed in suspicion. A dark shape loomed just beyond the reach of the dim light cast through broken windows. It wasn't often that he got summoned to places like this, and he hated it. The shadows were still, and the silence seemed almost deliberate, like a held breath.

From the darkness, a voice rang out, cold and clear, "You're needed by the Hoodie Assassin."

Claw Fist's jaw tightened, his fists clenching instinctively. "Why would he need me?" His voice was a low rumble, and he stepped closer, straining to see who spoke.

"It's important," the voice answered smoothly. "You're needed."

He scowled. Something about the tone was off, and he could swear it had a softer edge than he expected. "You sound like a girl. Why are you hiding?"

There was a moment of silence, and then the figure stepped forward into the faint light. A young woman, full of confidence and challenge in her eyes, looked back at him. She crossed her arms, the slightest hint of a smirk on her lips as she said, "I am a girl," she looked unfazed as she continued, "And I'm not scared."

Claw Fist tilted his head, studying her. "Hmm," he said with a raised brow, "you look pretty." His tone was as much a warning as a compliment. "And I'd rather not hurt you."

Kacey's smirk grew, "I'd love to see you try."

With a grunt, Claw Fist swung a punch, powerful enough to knock out any normal opponent. But Kacey moved in a blur, dodging his strikes with infuriating ease. She darted around him, weaving and ducking, always a step ahead.

"Stand still, would you?" Claw Fist growled, his movements growing more aggressive as his frustration mounted.

"I haven't even hit you yet," Kacey taunted, sidestepping another punch and retaliating with a well-placed kick. Her foot slammed into his side, and he staggered, caught off guard by her strength. She didn't stop there; her attacks came swift and merciless, each one landing with precision and power.

"What the...?" Claw Fist stumbled back, trying to catch his breath. "How?!" he screamed in frustration.

She paused, a calm and confident glint in her eye. "I'm powerful," she said, her voice steady as she stepped closer, unfazed by his size or reputation.

That was when Claw Fist made his move. He extended his claws, sharp as razors, and drove them into her stomach in one brutal strike. Kacey doubled over, blood trickling from her mouth, and a triumphant grin spread across his face.

"Now we know who's powerful," he said, pulling his claws back and watching as she stumbled.

But Kacey surprised him yet again. She straightened slowly, the blood disappearing, the wound closing as though it had never existed. Claw Fist's eyes widened, confusion breaking through his confident facade.

"How…?" he asked again, but slower this time, looking like he was shaken to the core.

Kacey met his stunned gaze. "I have a greater power than you, and you should respect that," she said, her tone calm and unwavering. Her words struck a nerve, and Claw Fist felt an unusual twinge of fear.

He roared in defiance, lunging at her with his claws again, desperate to reassert his dominance. But Kacey was ready. She sidestepped his attack, then swiftly pulled out a length of rope. In a deft movement, she wrapped it around him, binding his arms and legs before he could even register what was happening.

"Let me go!" Claw Fist bellowed, straining against the rope, his muscles bulging as he tried to break free. His claws scraped against the rope, but it was futile.

"Don't even think about cutting through it," Kacey said, a note of amusement in her voice. "It's uncuttable."

Claw Fist stopped struggling, glaring at her, "Why are you even doing this to me? I've done nothing wrong!"

Kacey leaned down, her face mere inches from his. "We need your help," she said simply. Without another word, she raised her hand and struck him sharply on the temple. His vision blurred, and he slumped forward, the world fading around him.

"That was dead easy," she muttered, a wry smile tugging at her lips as she straightened, brushing the dust off her hands.

Chapter 19

Jark leaned back in the driver's seat, his fingers tapping the wheel absentmindedly. The soft hum of the car was the only sound between him and San after they left the restaurant. They hadn't spoken much after their meal, but that was about to change.

"I hate the fact that the food at the restaurant is not good enough," San muttered, breaking the silence.

Jark glanced over with a slight smirk, "It was an African restaurant. What do you expect?"

"Wow, their food has too much seasoning," San retorted, his tone both incredulous and playful.

"I'll be frank with you," Jark replied, turning the car into their neighborhood. "I actually like a lot of seasoning in my food. It makes it, you know, taste like something."

San snorted but didn't respond, letting the topic drift away as they parked the car in front of Jark's place. Jark stepped out first, stretching his arms over his head. The night was calm, and the cool air hit him with a refreshing clarity. He glanced at his house, its dim lights casting long shadows in the yard.

"I wonder if she's even in the house," Jark mused as he approached the door.

San followed close behind. "She has-"

Before he could finish, the door swung open, revealing Kacey standing in the entryway, her usual sharp look softened by a warm smile.

"Welcome back, guys. I was just trying to figure out how to get you two back here," she said, stepping aside to let them in.

As they walked inside, Jark's eyes immediately narrowed when another figure stepped forward from behind Kacey. It was Claw Fist, the brawler who had tried to kill him not too long ago.

"What the hell is he doing here?" Jark asked, his voice cold and hard.

"We have a mission, and we need his help," Kacey replied, her expression unreadable.

"But he literally tried to kill me," Jark protested, his fists clenching instinctively at his sides.

"Yes, but he's changed," Kacey insisted, stepping between the two men.

Jark's brows shot up, "How do you know? Did you fight him to make him change or, I don't know, control his mind?"

Kacey rolled her eyes, though there was a touch of humor in it. "Yes, we fought. And no, I didn't control his mind. He's here because he wants to help. We need him."

Jark's gaze flicked over to Claw Fist, his jaw still tense. The brawler stepped forward, hands raised in a gesture of peace.

"Don't worry, Jark. I've changed. I promise not to hurt anyone. We're on the same side now."

Reluctantly, Jark allowed himself to ease off the tension, though suspicion still burned in his eyes. "I'm trusting you on this, Kacey," he said without glancing her way.

"Good," Kacey said as they all entered the house, "Oh, and don't forget to head to the dining room."

Jark let out a dry laugh, "That place hasn't been used in years."

But they all followed Kacey's lead, making their way to the dining table, which had been set with plates and simple dishes. The atmosphere felt odd, as though a storm were brewing right beneath the calm surface.

"We're here today to feast," Kacey began as they all sat down, "Before we leave for Nigeria."

Jark glanced at her, surprise flickering across his face, "Nigeria? Why are we going there?"

"We have some people to save," Kacey replied cryptically, avoiding eye contact as she started serving the food.

"Yeah, and I had to join by all means," Claw Fist chimed in, suddenly removing his mask.

Jark froze. His eyes widened in disbelief as he stared at the familiar face that had been hidden behind Claw Fist's disguise. "Kadrea!"

San, sitting beside Jark, looked just as shocked, his jaw nearly dropping. "I thought you were dead," he muttered, staring at Kadrea.

"Well, I was supposed to be…" Kadrea said, his voice was tinged with regret.

Jark felt a rush of memories floods back, the confusion he felt when Kadrea died – or rather, when he was made to kill her by the hoodie. A flashback hit him like a wave, the day they found Kadrea's body behind the college, the moment Jark had pulled him away from their group, hoping to see what Kadrea knew about his uncle's death, then Kadrea's confirmation that he knew what Jark was, and then the aftermath that led to Jark faking his own death. It all began to swirl in his mind, an old wound torn open once again.

The room fell into silence as Kadrea's presence hung heavy in the air. Jark's heart raced as the memories consumed him.

"What happened?" Jark asked softly.

Kadrea's eyes flashed as he started, "Well…"

*********FLASHBACK*********

Kadrea lay still in the casket, his breathing shallow as he listened to the voices above. He could barely make out the muffled conversation between two men he didn't know, but every word sent a chill through him. The grave had been opened, his supposed death was just a part of their twisted plan.

"What makes you think he's dead?" Danse's voice was sharp.

"Well, he's in the casket, and he's about to be buried," Gera replied, the sound of the grave shifting above.

Kadrea's heart pounded as Danse held up the Bradea claws.

"He does our dirty work while we focus on Plan B," Danse said, sealing Kadrea's fate as a pawn in their dangerous game.

*********END OF FLASHBACK*********

Jark stared at Kadrea, guilt weighing heavily on him as he spoke. "Later on, they claimed I was out of control and left me alone. I couldn't even show my family my face because they would think I was a demon," Kadrea said, his voice laced with pain.

"I'm sorry, Kadrea," Jark replied, his heart twisting, "It wasn't me. It was the suit that Kacey – or maybe Tabitha – forced me to wear."

Kadrea's expression softened, and he gave a small nod, "I've forgiven you, Jark. Let's just kick these bad guys' butts."

Relief washed over Jark, and he couldn't help but crack a smile.

119

"Okay, so what's the plan? We need money to get to Nigeria," Kadrea said, shifting the conversation forward.

"I have the money," Jark said quickly, eager to help.

San, leaning against the wall, smirked. "Why spend money when you have a genius right here?"

Jark blinked, then chuckled, "Oh yeah, you're right."

Kacey raised an eyebrow, glancing at San, and asked, "We have two days. You sure you can get that done?"

San crossed his arms confidently, "Of course, I can. Just sit back and watch."

Jark couldn't help but feel a spark of hope in the midst of their chaotic lives.

Maybe things will get better after all.

Chapter 20

Two days later, Danse stood triumphantly in the heart of the small kingdom of Grastor. His voice echoed through the streets as he rode on an enormous leaf, floating above the crowd like a new emperor on a throne of nature itself.

"Me," Danse declared with a wide grin. "Bow to your new emperor!"

The citizens of Grastor, overwhelmed by the sudden change in leadership, hesitated for a moment before one of them, a vanguard seller holding up newspapers, spoke out nervously, "All hail the new king! Please, whatever you do, don't challenge the king!"

The streets buzzed with confusion and reluctant obedience, but Danse reveled in it. Everything was going according to his plan.

*********Two Days Earlier*********

"Finally, we've arrived in Grastor," Danse said, stepping off the dusty road and into the kingdom's gates. The village was small, its stone buildings weathered but sturdy, and its people were simple yet vigilant.

"Now I can finally have my vacation," Gera sighed, stretching lazily as if the entire mission was just a detour in his dream of leisure.

Danse shot him an impatient glare, "No holiday for you. We have a world to dominate."

"Ah, no," Gera groaned, clearly displeased with the shift in plans.

Suddenly, a group of people with spears in their hands approached, forming a protective line across the street. The air grew thick with tension. At the center of the line, the king of Grastor emerged, a regal figure with his 18-year-old daughter at his side.

"Dad, these people look like foreigners," the girl said, her sharp eyes studying Danse and Gera with curiosity.

"Yes, we are," Danse responded smoothly, his tone diplomatic as he and Gera bowed in unison, "And we came here strictly for business."

Gera, sensing Danse might say too much, quickly interjected, "Your Majesty, we've come here for a vacation. We are explorers who travel the world, doing research and experiencing new things. We've come to see how the people of your great culture live."

Danse shot Gera a look. "Are we supposed to even tell them why we're here?" he whispered through gritted teeth.

"I deeply apologize for my companion's behavior," Gera said with a forced smile, trying to smooth over any awkwardness.

The king, however, seemed amused rather than offended. "All is forgiven," he said, his deep voice calm and commanding, "I am King Aroriwo, and this is my daughter-"

"I'm Selena," the girl interrupted proudly, earning a disapproving glance from her father.

"No, that's not your name," the king corrected, a mix of sternness and affection in his voice.

"Dad, they're foreigners," Selena argued playfully, "And I've told you it's not bad to have an English name. Mom did, didn't she?"

The king hesitated for a moment, then sighed and nodded, "Yes, she did."

Selena smiled, satisfied with her small victory. "Also, we have a festival soon. We would be honored if you would join us."

Before Danse or Gera could respond, the king called out to his guards. "Guards!"

"Yes, Your Majesty?" the captain of the guard responded.

"Take these gentlemen to their rooms. Ensure they are treated with respect and given anything they ask for," the king instructed. His voice left no room for dissent as the guards promptly moved to guide Danse and Gera.

As they were escorted to their quarters, Danse glanced at Gera, a slow, calculating smile spreading across his face. The king's trust and hospitality were a perfect opportunity for what they had planned. This peaceful kingdom, with its naive rulers and unsuspecting people, was ripe for manipulation.

"That was too easy," Danse murmured under his breath.

Gera shrugged, "You know, it wouldn't kill you to just enjoy the festival."

Danse smirked, "Maybe later. But first, we have a kingdom to conquer."

***

"Dad, something about them doesn't feel right," Selena said, her voice low but insistent.

The king, already walking away, waved dismissively. "They are not from here. How would they not be strange?" he replied over his shoulder.

Selena watched her father go, unease stirring in her chest. Something about the newcomers, Danse and Gera, didn't sit well with her. But with no real evidence, her father's casual dismissal was all she got. She sighed and decided to seek solace in a place that brought her comfort.

She made her way to a secluded garden where a statue of her mother stood tall, overlooking the grave where she rested. Selena knelt before it, her heart heavy. "Dear Mum, I know you can't hear me, and you're probably enjoying your mansion in heaven," she said softly, "I'm just disturbing you, but please…don't forget about me. I've asked for help, for the Hoodie Assassin to be sent to us. Why are they delaying?" Tears brimmed in her eyes as she lay down on the grave, letting the weight of her sorrow take over.

As if in answer, a strong wind began to blow, stirring the leaves around her. Selena sat up in surprise as the gust revealed something strange, an old door covered in weeds. The writing on it read "Do Not Open" but it was written as, *Wo do reve a*, in their local language.

She stepped closer, her fingers brushing the ancient wood. "What is this?" she whispered, her heart racing.

Suddenly, a voice startled her. "Princess!" one of the guards called out, and she turned around in fear, her pulse quickening.

"What was that for?" she asked, trying to hide her alarm.

"Sorry, the king said I should look for you," the guard explained, bowing slightly.

"I'm coming," she replied, casting one last glance at the door before leaving with him. Behind them, the wind stirred again, and the writing on the door seemed to glow faintly in the fading light: **Wo do reve a.**

Danse sat on the edge of the bed in their modest hotel room, staring out of the window at the streets of Grastor. The village was far more developed than he had expected, a mix of traditional charm and subtle modern touches. "This place is more developed than I expected it to be," he remarked, his tone laced with mild surprise.

Gera, busy smoothing out the blanket on his bed, glanced up. "What do you mean by that?" he asked, raising an eyebrow. "You're just downgrading African culture," he added, shaking his head in disapproval.

Danse waved his hand dismissively. "Yeah, yeah, whatever. Let's just get what we came for and be done with it," he said impatiently, clearly not in the mood for a cultural debate.

"Aren't we supposed to blend in so we don't look suspicious?" Gera asked, throwing a pointed look at Danse. He was always the one to play the diplomat, thinking ahead of everyone else.

Danse grunted, realizing Gera was right. "Yeah, that's true," he said but before they could continue, a knock at the door interrupted their conversation.

Gera tensed, motioning for Danse to be ready. "I'll open it, but be prepared for anything," he whispered, moving cautiously toward the door. He opened it slowly, revealing two local tailors standing nervously in the hallway.

"Hi, sorry for disturbing you guys," one of the tailors began, his voice polite but hopeful. "We are the tailors for the community, and the king has asked us to inform you about the festival. You'd be required to wear native clothing, and we were wondering if you would be interested."

The second tailor chimed in eagerly, "Please agree. This is a chance for our work to go far."

The first tailor added quickly, "But, of course, it's up to you."

Gera started to reply, "Well…" but was abruptly cut off by Danse.

"No," Danse said curtly, his voice cold and dismissive.

Gera, flustered, shot Danse a frustrated look before turning back to the tailors. "A moment, please," he said, closing the door halfway. He turned on Danse, lowering his voice, "What is your problem? You can't take over a place without even trying out their things! We need to fit in."

Danse crossed his arms defiantly, "I know, but we have to decline. They probably have some god or superstition that can expose us."

Gera looked at him incredulously, "Since when did you start fearing gods? I thought you believed they were just statues made to keep humans in line."

Danse gritted his teeth, unwilling to admit the deeper layers of his unease. Finally, he said, "Fine, I just don't want to, okay?"

Gera sighed, clearly exasperated but not in the mood for a fight. "Okay," he muttered, before opening the door again.

The first tailor, sensing their hesitation, spoke up, "First, we don't have gods in that sense. We trust in the Almighty One in heaven, and second, you don't have to pay for the clothes."

The second tailor added, his tone almost pleading, "Please, it would really help me and my wife care for our children better. It's been a hard season."

Gera, always the empathetic one, softened, "I'd really appreciate the offer, but I don't think my friend here is interested."

The first tailor's eyes darted between them before he hesitated before saying, "Is it okay if we come in and take measurements anyway? Just in case?"

Gera gave Danse a questioning look, but Danse remained silent, his face expressionless. After a moment, Gera nodded. "Alright. Come in," he said, opening the door wider as the tailors stepped in. The atmosphere in the room shifted, tension lingering as Gera wondered what was going on in Danse's mind.

But Danse's thoughts were already elsewhere. They were on the plan, on the festival, and the dangers that might lurk behind Grastor's pleasant facade.

Chapter 21

The next day, Danse woke to a sight that momentarily caught him off guard. Colorful decorations were draped across the streets, vibrant lights flickering in a playful display. The entire village had transformed overnight for the festival.

"Wow, this is cool," Gera said, rubbing his eyes, "Remind me why we're supposed to dethrone the king again?"

Danse didn't even hesitate. "Because I need their secret weapon," he replied, his eyes scanning the festivities outside. "The Onowo powers," he added, almost as an afterthought.

Gera raised an eyebrow. "And what exactly is that?"

Danse shrugged, "I have no idea. Let's just find out when we get our hands on it."

Gera laughed. "While you obsess over secret weapons, I'll enjoy myself," With that, he grabbed his jacket and headed out to join the festivities.

***

Meanwhile, in the garage, Jark was getting restless. "Are you not done yet?" he asked, walking in with an impatient tone. The garage reeked of metal and fuel, the hum of tools buzzing in the background as San and Kacey worked on their escape plan.

"Does it look like he's done?" Kacey responded, barely looking up as she sipped from her drink. She sat casually against the workbench, watching the others fumble with equipment.

Kadrea, sitting nearby, wiped the sweat from his brow, "Even if we finish everything and it works perfectly, how are we going to get to them? We still don't have a solid plan."

Jark let out a small chuckle, "I guess you've really changed, huh, Kadrea? Getting all tactical now."

"Obviously. I literally accepted your half-assed apology, didn't I?" Kadrea shot back with a sarcastic smile.

San, who had been watching the two bicker from the side, piped up, "It wasn't that bad of an apology. I mean, he tried."

Jark threw his hands up defensively, "Look, it's not my fault you were acting like you never thought things through. I was just saying-"

"Enough!" Kacey's voice cut through the room like a whip. "You guys need to stop this childish nonsense. We're supposed to be working together, not squabbling like a bunch of kids." Her eyes blazed with frustration as she said, "This is bigger than us."

Kadrea rolled his eyes. "Yeah, well, I'm done with this crap." He stood up and began walking toward the exit. He left but not before saying, "If you need me, I'll be anywhere but here. Probably taking Sanja's car."

Jark shrugged and followed suit, "I'm going with him. This is getting ridiculous."

Kacey sighed, knowing she couldn't stop them, "Fine. Just make sure no one gets killed, okay? I'll follow to make sure you don't mess things up." She grabbed her jacket and marched after them, leaving the garage behind.

As the three walked off, San and the robotic assistant, Robant, remained in the garage. "I'm still amazed she's the only woman in this house and she's not afraid of any of us," San muttered, adjusting a wrench.

Robant's mechanical voice hummed, "Trust me, I've scanned her. She's dangerous."

San raised an eyebrow but didn't argue. He sighed and said, "Yeah, well, let's just get this jet fixed up so we can finally visit my best friend's homeland."

"You seem excited," Robant noted.

San paused, smiling to himself, "No, it's not that. I mean, yeah, it'll be cool, but I guess I just feel lucky. Helping heroes and all. But..." He trailed off, glancing at Robant's unblinking eyes.

"Please stop staring at me. It's not my fault," San said.

"I said nothing," Robant replied in monotone.

Meanwhile, Kadrea reached the car, his hand on the door when he heard footsteps behind him. His instincts kicked in, and he immediately spun around, claws at the ready. "Who's there?" he demanded.

"Chill, dude. It's just me," Jark said, stepping out from the shadows.

Kadrea relaxed a little, though his stance remained tense. "What, you want me to beat you up again?" His voice carried the weight of their shared past.

Jark gave him a half-smile, "I thought we were cool now?"

"We are," Kadrea sighed, "I was just messing with you."

"Then what was all that arguing about?"

Kadrea shook his head, "Nothing that matters."

Kacey arrived, hearing the tail end of their conversation. "Look, I know it's not easy to let go of the past," she said softly, "but I appreciate that you're willing to help us, Kadrea."

Kadrea shot her a pointed look, "Help? You practically forced me here."

Kacey chuckled, "At least you're with your friends again."

"Wait a minute," Jark interrupted, "You *forced* him to come?"

Kacey shifted uncomfortably, "Well, I wouldn't say 'forced' exactly..."

"Why are you always making people do stuff for you?" Jark asked, getting into the car with a raised eyebrow.

"Maybe I should work on making friends properly instead of pressuring them," Kacey mumbled to herself as she watched them drive off. She turned back to the garage, feeling a little self-conscious.

When she re-entered, San glanced up from his work. "What's wrong?" he asked.

"At least you're my friend," Kacey muttered.

San gave a sympathetic laugh. "I know someone who feels like that all the time."

"Who?"

"Jark," San said, his voice softening, "He hides it well, but he feels the same like he's not really accepted. You shouldn't feel bad about it. What matters is what you do about those feelings."

Kacey sat down next to him and asked, "Is that what made you become an engineer?"

San grinned. "No, not exactly. I just told myself, 'Sanja Le Franco Denay, why waste your life when you can be useful?' And here I am, helping out heroes."

"Wow, that's your full name?" Kacey asked, genuinely surprised.

"Yup. Used to hate it, but now, I'm cool with it."

Kacey smiled faintly, "I get that. I had to change my name so many times because of my powers."

"What's your real name, then?"

"It's actually Kacey. And also Tabitha. My mom let me use my real names once she felt I was mature enough."

San chuckled, "Wait, you had to change your hero name, too?"

Kacey groaned, "Yeah. My old one was... Barro."

San couldn't hold back his laughter, "I knew it."

She rolled her eyes, "It's terrible, isn't it?"

"Yeah, not great," San admitted, "You'll come up with something better." Then he added, "Speaking of names, why are we headed to Africa again?"

Kacey leaned back and explained, "We're going to save people from the ones who gave Kadrea his powers. My mother warned me about them."

"How do you know all this?"

"My mom told me before she-" Kacey paused. "Well, let's just say she's been guiding me."

San nodded slowly. "Then I guess we're all in this together."

Chapter 22

The streets of Grastor shimmered under the lights of the festival, shadows dancing in sync with the music filling the air. The King and Princess stood on the balcony, addressing the crowd as they poured their hearts into the speech, a call to honor both past and present lives, the people who had shaped Grastor and made sacrifices for it. Meanwhile, Danse and Gera slipped away, weaving through the alleys until they reached an unguarded side of the royal compound.

Danse crouched low, his eyes narrowing as he inspected a door leading to the room he'd heard whispers about. The room with "Wo do reve a" written in faded letters on the wall, rumored to hold secrets that no one else had ever been able to decipher. He heard the Princess's voice drifting over from the balcony.

"As we all know," Selena began, her voice steady, "this festival is not only for just celebration but for us to honor the ones who gave us life, the people who were always there to care for us." Her voice softened, "Even though mine has gone to join our elders in heaven, I pray that God continues to bless the ones who are still here with us."

With that, the crowd burst into applause as the music rose, drowning out the quiet murmur of Danse and Gera's stealthy footsteps. Gera seemed distracted, momentarily caught up in the revelry.

"I really like this," he said, glancing around, "What's it called again…uhm…"

"Stop," Danse cut him off, holding up his hand, "We're here."

Gera huffed, inspecting his traditional outfit as if he'd been greatly inconvenienced. "What was that for? Don't stain my native…Oh! That's what it's called," he said with a smirk, taking a mental note.

Danse raised an eyebrow, unfazed, "We're here."

Gera's eyes followed Danse's gesture to the wall, where faint letters seemed to flicker in the torchlight. "What are we looking at, exactly?" he asked.

"This," Danse replied, pointing to the faded words, "**Wo do reve a**."

"Alright, so…how do we get in?" Gera asked, squinting at the wall as if it would reveal its secrets.

Danse reached into his satchel and pulled out a worn, leather-bound book. He flipped through the pages until he found the passage he'd painstakingly translated, "All we need is this."

Gera raised an eyebrow and asked, "What is that?"

Danse let out a dry chuckle, "Wow, Gera, that is the most intelligent question you've asked me all night."

Gera rolled his eyes, "Really?"

"Yes. Now shut up and stay in that corner," Danse said, positioning himself in front of the wall. He held the book up, reading from it slowly, each word seeming to echo against the walls of the quiet room. "Rovie rōkomē eware ididi na sino hotō Ōnowo sir obō no ogaga ra komē mē reē te rehiē ru oware nō orē wha erere."

The air grew thick and cold, and a low hum filled the room. Symbols on the wall began to glow, casting an eerie, pale light that danced across Danse's face. Both men tensed as whispering voices filled the air, indistinct and unsettling.

"What…what are they saying?" Gera stammered, rubbing his arms against a sudden chill, "It doesn't even sound like anything these people speak."

Danse didn't answer, his eyes fixed on the wall as it began to shift. Stone by stone, a passage opened before them, the air thick with the smell of old earth and ancient secrets. They stepped inside cautiously, their gazes falling upon a bracelet perched atop a pile of rocks, gleaming even in the dim light. The bracelet appeared ordinary, but Danse sensed something potent in its presence, a faint energy humming from it like a heartbeat.

Danse took a step forward, reaching toward the bracelet, only to be pulled back sharply by Gera's grip on his shoulder.

"Wait!" Gera's voice was a harsh whisper, "What if it's a trap?"

Danse glanced over, frustration flashing in his eyes, though he couldn't deny the possibility. Gera's caution had saved them before. He looked back at the bracelet, weighing his next move. The voices around them grew louder, but the words remained unintelligible. The air was thick with tension and a sense of foreboding, pressing in on them.

"This place was built to protect its secrets," Danse murmured, almost to himself, "But that doesn't mean it'll keep them from us."

He reached into his satchel again, pulling out a thin metal rod and holding it close to the bracelet, "You might be right, Gera. But there's only one way to find out."

He inched the rod toward the bracelet, and as it brushed against the surface, a faint blue spark flashed, and the room trembled. Danse tensed, but he didn't pull back. The voices were a symphony of haunting tones, almost like a song, filling his mind with images he couldn't understand. Yet.

"We came here for this," Danse said firmly, turning to Gera, "Trap or not, it's ours now."

Gera glanced from Danse to the bracelet, a flicker of both fear and awe in his eyes, "Fine, but if we get cursed, I'm holding you responsible."

Danse smirked, stepping forward, "Then you better start praying."

***

The festival lights sparkled around Selena, casting a warm glow over the crowded square as her father, the King, stood beside her on the balcony. Laughter and cheers filled the air, but Selena couldn't shake the feeling that something was wrong. An invisible tension prickled at the edge of her senses, creeping down her spine and coiling in her gut.

She turned to her father, her voice quiet yet urgent as she said, "Dad, there is something wrong."

The King looked at her, his face softening with a smile as he waved to the people below. "What is it, Yole?" he asked, using the childhood nickname she had long outgrown, "It's a wonderful day! What could possibly be wrong?"

Selena's eyes narrowed. "I told you not to call me that," she snapped, frustration clear in her voice. "And I can feel it…there's something not right."

"Stop that and enjoy the day," the King replied, giving her shoulder a light pat as if dismissing her concerns as a passing whim.

"Fine," she said, exasperated, "You can keep on being naïve about what I feel, or you could come with me to find out what's wrong."

The King just laughed gently, shaking his head, "My dear, let's just enjoy the day as it is."

"Fine," she said, stepping back as her father returned his attention to the crowd. She let out a long sigh, feeling the sharp sting of dismissal in her chest. "Why is he so stubbornly ignorant?" she muttered to herself. "I've told him I have powers, or something close to it, but he just keeps denying it. Maybe it's not magic, but how does he explain the things I sense?"

She walked away from the balcony, navigating the palace halls until she reached a secluded passage. Her steps quickened, led by the feeling she could no longer ignore, and it pulled her toward a place she had found before but did not have the chance to see what it really was.

It was a room with a door where the phrase "Wo do reve a" was scrawled on the surface. She reached the doorway and froze, her eyes widening. The door, which should have been locked, was slightly open.

"Oh no…this is a catastrophe," she whispered, heart racing as she spun around to alert someone. Before she could take a step, a strong hand grabbed her wrist, yanking her back.

"Help! Someone, help me!" she cried, struggling against the grip.

As she was pulled into the shadows, she managed to catch sight of her captor's face under the dim light. Her eyes narrowed in recognition, shock blending with betrayal, "Gera? How could you?"

Gera avoided her gaze, his face flushed, "I'm sorry, Your Highness, but Danse ordered me to bring you."

Selena huffed and yanked her arm free, glaring at him, "Alright, fine, but do you mind not grabbing me like that?"

"Sorry, my Highness," Gera mumbled, leading her down the narrow corridor until they reached a room where Danse was waiting, seated casually as if he owned the place.

"Oh, welcome, Princess," Danse said, flashing a smile as if they were old friends, "I need your help with something."

Selena crossed her arms, glaring down at him, "And why should I help you? You obviously know I won't, because I don't trust either of you."

She turned to leave, but Gera moved to block her path. "Hey, move," she said, her voice raised, "Get out of my way!"

Gera hesitated, his expression conflicted, but he didn't budge. Danse leaned forward, his tone softer, "I'm sorry, Princess, but I need you to work with us so we don't make a wrong choice here."

"I would never," she hissed, trying to push past Gera again.

Before she could continue, a strange fog crept into her mind. The room began to blur, spinning around her like the lights of the festival outside. She staggered, confusion clouding her vision. "What... ha... ve... you... do..." she murmured, her words slurring as her eyelids grew heavy.

Danse's voice echoed dimly in her ears, but his words were lost in the haze. Her legs felt like lead, and she stumbled, fighting to keep her eyes open. With a final, stifled gasp, her vision went dark, and she fell into the unknown.

Chapter 23

Later, Selena slowly opened her eyes, disoriented and trying to get her bearings. Her vision cleared to reveal Danse, watching her with a gleam of satisfaction.

"You're awake. Finally, we can get started with you now," Danse said with a casual smirk.

Selena struggled against her restraints, her voice hoarse when she asked, "What did you do to me?"

"Nothing much," Danse replied, feigning innocence, "Just gave you a little rest from all that stress." He leaned in, his eyes gleaming with intent. "Now, do you mind telling me how to activate these powers?"

Selena glared at him, her defiance momentarily faltering as words escaped her mouth almost involuntarily, "Doresto hend piaer Mangde..."

Realizing she had spoken, her eyes widened, "What... what did you do to me?"

Danse chuckled, slipping a bracelet on his wrist as power surged through him, "Nothing. You did it all on your own."

As he reveled in the energy coursing through him, he used a vine to bind Selena and suspended her above the ground. "Now you'll hang there while I take care of your kingdom," he sneered.

With that, he and Gera left the room, leaving Selena trapped and helpless.

***

Jark leaned against the cold metal wall of the plane, his heart racing with anticipation. "Can't it go any faster? We have people that need to be saved!" The urgency in his voice echoed in the cramped cabin, filled with the distinct hum of engines straining against the sky.

San, seated at the controls, shot him a glance, his brow furrowed. "Well, this is as fast as it can go," he replied, his voice steady but tinged with frustration.

Kadrea, who sat nearby, leaned forward, a mischievous glint in his eye. "What about this button?" he asked, reaching out to press a bright red button on the console. In an instant, the plane jolted to a standstill in mid-air, the cabin filling with shocked silence.

"Look what you've done!" San shouted, his voice rising in panic as the plane trembled ominously.

"Uh, not to disturb your disagreement," Kacey interjected, her tone urgent, "but there's something going on."

Jark's stomach dropped as he felt a strange shift in the air. "Yeah, I feel it too," he muttered, a sense of dread creeping over him. Just then, the plane suddenly surged forward, gaining an unexpected boost of energy, and within moments, they were soaring through the sky once more. The rush of wind filled the cabin as they approached their destination, but just as they neared the coast of Grastor, the engines sputtered and the plane abruptly descended, crashing into the water with a heavy splash.

"Great landing!" Kadrea quipped, his voice dripping with sarcasm as they scrambled to escape the sinking vessel. "Sorry about that," he added, sheepishly avoiding eye contact.

"How are you going to get it out?" Kacey asked, her brow raised in concern as they waded through the water, the plane now a submerged wreck behind them.

"Don't worry. Robant will do that," San assured them, his eyes scanning the horizon as they made their way to the entrance of the city.

As they stepped onto the shore, the city of Grastor unfolded before them, beautifully designed and adorned with vibrant flowers that lined the pathways. A grand archway welcomed them, its inscription written in an unfamiliar language. "Firanco," it read, meaning "welcome."

"What language do you guys actually speak here?" San asked, bewildered. "It's not like any language I've seen before."

Kacey shrugged, brushing a flower petal from her shoulder. "Well, my mum told me they called it animal language so people wouldn't want to study it, but I'm not really sure of the real name," she explained as they walked further in.

As they ventured deeper, Jark's heart sank at the sight of devastation. Vines twisted and choked the once-thriving gardens, their tendrils clawing at the city like a living nightmare.

"What happened here?" Kadrea asked, a sense of urgency lacing his words. Just then, a guard stumbled toward them, his uniform torn and his face pale.

"Yes! Finally, God has sent us a helper!" the guard exclaimed, falling to his knees before them, desperation etched across his features.

"Oh no, this is a disaster," Kacey murmured, her voice trembling. "Where is the king?"

"He is in their custody," the guard replied, his voice quaking as a vine coiled around his chest, squeezing tightly.

"Well, well, well," a mocking voice cut through the tension. "If it isn't the Hoodie Assassin and Claw Fist, and who is she? Not that it matters, because we're still going to kill you all anyway." Danse emerged from the shadows, a sinister grin on his face as a vine writhed in the air, ready to strike at San.

In a flash, the vine lunged, but Jark reacted instinctively, shouting, "No!" as he lunged forward, trying to intervene. The vine was sliced off mid-air, falling harmlessly to the ground.

"You're quick but not for long," Danse taunted, his eyes narrowing as he prepared for another attack.

"Now let these people go!" Jark demanded, his voice steady despite the chaos swirling around them.

"No way! I can't! I need their powers to rule the world, especially those that said I could never become anything!" Danse sneered, his ambition twisted and vile.

Kacey stepped forward, determination shining in her eyes. "Here's the plan: you two have to work together and distract him while we go find the king," she instructed urgency guiding her words.

"Hey!" Danse shouted, frustration bubbling over as he tried to restrain them with the vines. But just as they began to bind Jark and San, Claw Fist intervened, slicing through the tendrils with a swift motion.

"Go quickly!" Claw Fist urged, his voice booming as the fight intensified around them. Jark felt the adrenaline surge through him, and for a moment, everything else faded away. It was time to fight back, to reclaim what was theirs, and to save those who needed them most.

"I thought they were the last people we were going to fight! How come he was ready for us?" San gasped between breaths, frustration lacing his voice as they ran away from where the fight was happening.

"It appears they must have been expecting us," Kacey interjected, her expression serious as they navigated the ruins. "But right now, we need to find the princess. I want you to get out of here because you can easily get killed."

San stopped, leaning against a crumbling wall to catch his breath. "But…I…can…One minute." He inhaled deeply, regaining his composure. "But I can help!" he insisted, determination shining in his eyes. "I know I can!"

"If you can, then find the princess or the king," Kacey said teasingly, though her concern was evident. "Look, San, I know you've helped a lot, but we cannot risk you dying. This is one of the tools our ancient fathers used to fight, and it is stronger than any human's comprehension." She tried to explain, but San shook his head defiantly.

"I won't leave, even if it means I end here!" he shouted, a fierce resolve igniting within him.

Just then, a faint voice echoed through the air, barely audible yet full of desperation. "Yes, help us," it called out, the tone low and distant. San's heart leaped as he turned to Kacey. "I think I can locate the sound from where it is coming from," he said. "Tadao!" He scanned the area, focusing until he pinpointed its origin and said, "It's coming from inside the palace!"

"We can't just go in. It's dangerous," Kacey cautioned, her voice tense.

"It isn't," San countered, his eyes darting toward the imposing structure. "He doesn't really have any guards. Most of them are frightened, and many are dead." He scanned the building, his expression grim. "I see two bodies at the bottom of the tower."

"Really hope it's the king and her daughter," Kacey murmured, anxiety creeping into her voice. "How do we get in?"

"Through the back," San replied, pointing toward an entrance partially concealed by debris. They hurried to the entrance and slipped inside, hearts pounding as they entered the dimly lit corridor.

As they made their way through the palace, they soon discovered the source of the voice. There, chained and vulnerable, was the princess, her face pale but strikingly beautiful. "Please, leave me! Save my father! Danse wants to kill him, and I don't really know why!" Selena cried, her eyes wide with fear.

"Oh my gosh, she looks very pretty," San blurted out, a blush creeping onto his cheeks. Both Kacey and Selena turned to stare at him in disbelief. "Wait, did I say that out? No! I'm just kidding...not like that...uh, I was-"

"Forget about that and take the princess out of here while I go get her father!" Kacey said, urgency in her tone as she rubbed her sore wrists, still raw from the chains.

Suddenly, the door crashed open, and Danse stormed in, flinging Jark and Kadrea's bodies to the floor. "You think you guys can stop me?" he taunted, a wicked grin spreading across his face as he prepared to attack.

***

The battle had raged on after San and Kacey had left. Danse had been relentless, striking with deadly precision. Jark and Kadrea struggled to catch their breath, the weight of their exhaustion bearing down on them. "Now I will show you my true power!" Danse roared, his blade flashing as he stabbed at them repeatedly. They felt their strength waning, the world fading to darkness as they succumbed to his relentless assault.

***

"No!" San cried, rushing to their side as he knelt beside the fallen. "How could you kill them? They're just kids!" Tears streamed down his face, grief mingling with rage.

"Oh, sorry we're late," Jark said, his voice coming from behind Danse and San froze as Jark continued to say, "We realized he tried to spoil our plan, so we did it before him. While he hit us away, I was able to make clones like the previous assassin did, and we followed your tracks."

"We need to get to the room where he got it from," Selena urged, her voice trembling with determination as she came to a stand beside Jark.

"How do we do that?" Kadrea asked, glancing nervously around the dim chamber as the walls echoed with impending doom.

"I don't know. Let's just try something; it's below us!" Selena exclaimed, pointing to a trapdoor beneath their feet.

As if summoned by their desperation, Danse began to attack again, his rage palpable. Kacey quickly conjured a force field around the princess and San, shielding them from his fury while Jark and Claw Fist engaged in a fierce fight against Danse's relentless strikes.

"You will soon be tired, and I will finally get what I want!" Danse sneered, his confidence unwavering.

Just then, Gera walked into the room and said, "Danse, the people are asking for their king!"

"Why now?" he snarled, frustration boiling over as the onslaught paused momentarily.

"Now!" Jark shouted, seizing the opportunity. The ground beneath them trembled, and in an instant, the floor exploded, sending debris flying as they all fell into the darkness below. Jark braced himself for impact, the chaos around him blurring into a cacophony of sounds and sensations. They were plunging into the unknown, but one thought burned brightly in his mind: they had to find a way to stop Danse, reclaim the throne, and save the kingdom. Failure was not an option.

As they tumbled into the hidden room, Jark quickly regained his footing, his eyes scanning the dim space. Ancient symbols glowed faintly on the walls, each pulsating with a strange energy.

"Stay alert, everyone," he called, his voice tense but steady. "This is where he's drawing his power."

Kadrea brushed the dust off himself, his eyes gleaming with excitement and determination, "Finally, we're getting to the root of all this."

Selena stepped forward, her eyes narrowing as she examined the inscriptions. "These markings...they tell a story. This place isn't just a source of power; it's a prison."

"A prison?" Kacey asked, puzzled.

Selena nodded grimly, "Yes. A powerful being was sealed here, and Danse must have found a way to tap into it."

Danse's laughter echoed from above as he descended, his face illuminated with sinister delight, "You all found my little secret, but it's too late to stop me now."

Jark's fists clenched as he prepared for what was bound to be their final battle, "We'll see about that."

Chapter 24

Jark stood amidst the chaos, breathless and battered, watching as Danse unleashed another wave of attacks. "What kind of weak attack is this?" Danse sneered, his voice dripping with disdain. He pointed his hand, summoning vines that lashed out, only to realize something was wrong. The energy he wielded was faltering; two crucial components were missing – his wrist and the bracelet that amplified his powers, both severed in their last encounter.

"How could you cut off my wrist? Was that really necessary?" Danse grimaced, a mix of pain and anger flickering across his face, yet a cruel grin remained as he glared at Gera, who stood nearby.

"Sorry, master," Gera mumbled, extending his arms in a reluctant hug, only to be shoved aside by Danse, who was now frantically searching for his lost appendages. In the midst of the tension, Selena began to chant softly, recalling words she had heard her mother speak during her childhood.

"Sorlemly universe belipate," she said, her voice quivering with uncertainty. Suddenly, the world around them twisted, and they were transported to a different arena. Everything was a stark red, the soil, the hills, the mountains, except for the sky, which was a sickly yellow hue.

"Where are we?" San asked, his eyes darting around in shock.

"This is the universe of the tools we use," Kacey replied, her tone serious. "Why did you bring us here?"

"I had no idea what the spell does! I just said it!" Selena exclaimed, panic rising in her voice.

"It's not a spell; it means it takes us to the true form of the tools," Kacey clarified, her gaze fixed on the shifting landscape.

"Oh no," Selena gasped, realizing the implications. Suddenly, Danse vanished, along with Gera, leaving them in a realm that felt increasingly hostile.

"What happened?" Jark asked, a knot tightening in his stomach.

"It's getting rid of everything that doesn't belong here," Kacey explained, watching as the environment trembled ominously. Selena, glancing down, noticed the bracelet shimmering on the ground. She quickly picked it up, and at that moment, a portal opened before them.

Selena walked through it but then immediately came back inside to exclaim, "It is the real world, let's get out!"

Just as they prepared to escape, laughter echoed through the red arena. "You did not really think I was going to let you go, did you?" Kadrea taunted as he transformed into his true form, a grotesque creature floating above him. Jark felt his own power surge as an octopus-like being emerged from him, its tentacles writhing in the air.

"If that's how you want to play it, then let's end this," Jark said, clenching his fists, ready for a fight.

"We need to get out of here! We don't know what could happen to us!" Kacey urged, fear lacing her words. "Legends say this is the place where these tools reveal themselves if the wielder hasn't mastered them."

"Then the legend is wrong, because I knew this was the only place I could defeat the Hoodie Assassin, and that's why I played along," Kadrea replied, his eyes glinting with malice as he prepared for combat.

"I know Jark, and he wouldn't want to do this!" San shouted, desperation creeping into his voice. Jark remained silent, his focus sharpening as he prepared for the inevitable clash.

Minutes passed, and the ground began to tremble violently. The portal that had offered them an escape was starting to close. "We need to leave!" Kacey shouted, her urgency rising.

"What about them?" San asked, his eyes flickering between Kadrea and Jark.

"No time again! Let's just go!" Kacey insisted, grabbing San's arm and pulling him toward the closing portal. But San hesitated, glancing back one last time before the boulder landed in the portal's path, sealing it shut.

"Wow, this place is beautiful!" San exclaimed, his awe cutting through the tension.

"How did this happen?" Kacey asked, confused as she looked around.

"It was the bracelet," a voice interjected, drawing their attention. The king emerged from the shadows, his presence commanding.

"Dad!" Selena cried, rushing to embrace him. She pulled back, her expression shifting from joy to suspicion. "Wait, how did you know?"

"I'm sorry, my love. I should have told you sooner. Your mother was the one who wore it and used it to save the kingdom. After the Bradaetha and Kaderian were lost, this bracelet was the last one of the four that remained," the king explained, his voice heavy with regret.

"The Four!" they exclaimed in unison, their minds racing with the implications.

"There are four?" Kacey asked, incredulous.

"Yes. As the guards, you are supposed to find them all and retrieve them so that peace in Africa can be restored. Did Ciara not tell you this?" The king looked at them with a mixture of hope and concern.

"No, my lord," Kacey admitted, her voice low.

"Your mother and I need to do our jobs well," the king said, his gaze piercing.

"Then why am I involved?" Jark interjected, feeling the weight of their expectations shift onto him. Before he could voice his fears, San and Kacey hugged him tightly, the warmth of their friendship grounding him.

"Chill out, I'm fine," Jark said, trying to downplay his anxiety, but the seriousness of the moment loomed large.

"What happened?" San asked, a brief flashback flickering in Jark's mind, igniting memories of their struggles.

***

"I wouldn't leave you here to die," Jark said, gritting his teeth as he strained against the boulder pinning Claw Fist.

"Wait! Can't I just use my claws?" Claw Fist replied, panic rising in his voice as he struggled beneath the weight.

"I'm starting to lose my breath! Quickly, get help!"

The pressure intensified, and Jark felt helpless as the boulder pressed down harder. Desperation surged within him, and he turned to find assistance, but a falling rock struck him on the head, plunging him into darkness.

When Jark finally opened his eyes, he felt the roughness of the ground beneath him and saw a girl dragging him along. He blinked, momentarily disoriented, then closed his eyes again, slipping in and out of consciousness as she washed his face, hands, and feet. With a final gasp, he awoke fully and found himself behind the palace, the world around him spinning into focus.

***

They were now in the king's palace, the grandeur surrounding them both awe-inspiring and intimidating. Jark's voice broke the silence. "Now can I know why I was involved?"

The king looked at him, a mixture of pride and regret in his eyes. "My son, I don't really have an answer for you. But I'm happy that we found the bracelet, and it was restored back to us." Jark felt a surge of confusion and determination hoping to find out why things had turned out like this one day.

Epilogue

Years later, the Gastro Kingdom was back to normal, its vibrant streets bustling with life. However, some developments took unexpected turns. For one, Selena had ascended to the throne at just 20 years old, her relationship with San blooming alongside her royal responsibilities. Kacey and Jark, on the other hand, faced a different kind of adventure; Jark was determined to uncover the identity of the fourth wearer of the powerful bracelet and to understand the mysterious figure that haunted his dreams. As for Kadrea, they hoped never to see him again.

In the Tool Verse, Kadrea found himself trapped beneath a massive boulder, the weight pressing down on him. "How can I get out of here? I need to leave!" he grunted, straining to push himself up as his creature, an odd, floating entity, attempted to assist him.

"Hwmwsuwso," the creature uttered, its voice soothing, meaning, "We are friends, not supposed to fight."

"Sorry, I don't speak creature! Please leave me alone," Kadrea snapped, frustration bubbling to the surface as he searched desperately for a way out.

Meanwhile, in a void of nothingness, Danse and Gera floated, trapped in a space devoid of time or matter. The silence was oppressive, amplifying the tension between them.

"Because of you, we failed," Danse said, his voice cold and accusatory.

"I'm sorry, my love! I only did it because I loved you!" Gera protested, voice filled with desperation.

"No, I am-" he began, but then a memory flashed before him, illuminating his mind with startling clarity. As visions of the past cascaded through his thoughts, everything fell into place.

To Be Continued............

The Battle of the Heart

In the depths of our being, there lies an eternal struggle – a battle of the heart that only those with unwavering resolve can hope to conquer. The heart, often perceived merely as an organ that sustains life, functions on a far deeper level than we might initially comprehend. It is the seat of our emotions, the wellspring of our desires, and the compass that guides our moral decisions. Engaging in this battle requires not just strength but also a profound commitment to what is right, both within ourselves and in alignment with a higher purpose or divine will.

The Call to Battle

At times, we find ourselves at a crossroads, needing a catalyst to propel us into action. This push can come from unexpected quarters – an event, a person, or even an inner revelation – that challenges us to confront our deepest fears and aspirations. This impetus can lead us down paths we never anticipated, revealing opportunities for growth or pitfalls of temptation. The crucial question then becomes: how do we respond when faced with such choices?

Choosing the Right Path

Consider the story of Jark, who found himself in a situation where he felt he had no other option but to proceed down a certain path. He said, "I have no other option, so I just went ahead." This response reflects a sense of resignation and inevitability that many of us might feel when confronted with difficult decisions. However, it also highlights the importance of agency and choice in shaping our destinies.

Alternatively, imagine choosing to be the best version of yourself by affirming: "No matter how powerful I am, I will always strive to do what is right." This mindset embodies the essence of integrity and moral courage. It requires us to stand firm in our convictions, even when the easier path might lead us astray.

The Role of Faith and Willpower

Winning the battle of the heart often involves aligning our actions with our beliefs and values. For those who hold faith as a guiding principle, this alignment includes seeking guidance from God or a higher power. It is through this connection that we find strength and clarity to navigate life's complexities.

Moreover, cultivating a strong will is essential. It empowers us to resist temptations and make choices that reflect our true selves rather than succumbing to external pressures or fleeting desires.

Conclusion

In conclusion, the battle of the heart is an ongoing journey – a testament to our resilience and capacity for growth. Whether we are propelled by an external push or an internal drive, the choices we make define who we are and who we aspire to become. By committing to what is right and nurturing our relationship with ourselves and with God, we can emerge victorious in this profound struggle. Let us strive to be individuals who choose integrity over convenience and righteousness over complacency.

Printed in Great Britain
by Amazon

61072080R00097